SILENCE INTERRUPTED

ALSO BY HELEN WESTON

The Winter is Past
It is Solved by Walking

SILENCE INTERRUPTED

A silent retreat takes a dark turn

HELEN WESTON

T

Copyright © 2024 Helen Weston

The moral right of the author has been asserted.

Apart from any fair dealing for the purposes of research or private study, or criticism or review, as permitted under the Copyright, Designs and Patents Act 1988, this publication may only be reproduced, stored or transmitted, in any form or by any means, with the prior permission in writing of the publishers, or in the case of reprographic reproduction in accordance with the terms of licences issued by the Copyright Licensing Agency. Enquiries concerning reproduction outside those terms should be sent to the publishers.

This is a work of fiction. Names, characters, businesses, places, events and incidents are either the products of the author's imagination or used in a fictitious manner. Any resemblance to actual persons, living or dead, or actual events is purely coincidental.

Troubador Publishing Ltd
Unit E2 Airfield Business Park,
Harrison Road, Market Harborough,
Leicestershire LE16 7UL
Tel: 0116 279 2299
Email: books@troubador.co.uk
Web: www.troubador.co.uk

ISBN 978 1 80514 318 5

British Library Cataloguing in Publication Data.
A catalogue record for this book is available from the British Library.

Printed and bound in Great Britain by CMP UK
Typeset in 10.5pt Adobe Garamond Pro by Troubador Publishing Ltd, Leicester, UK

For Wendy,
who made it possible to think about these things

*The summer's flower is to the summer sweet
Though to itself it only live and die,
But if that flower with base infection meet,
The basest weed outbraves his dignity:
For sweetest things turn sourest by their deeds;
Lilies that fester smell far worse than weeds.*

Extract from Sonnet 94 by William Shakespeare

CHAPTER ONE

The high wall was intimidating, as it was meant to be. It wrapped around the house, so that you couldn't see it from the road, only from the river, looking up. The house was right on the city wall, on the edge of the medieval quarter, built as a fortified manor house against the raids of the Scots. The only way in was through a side gate in a steep, narrow street.

Lizzie hesitated, her hand on the latch of the heavy, metal gate, still unsure if it was a good idea to return after so long, but the muscles around her heart ached with the effort of pushing down the memories that lockdown had brought to the surface. So, when the retreat was advertised, she had booked it quickly before she could change her mind and made the journey from the shelter of her mountain, eastwards to Penrith, then up the motorway to the ancient border city.

Mustering her courage, she pushed open the gate and walked into the tranquil walled garden that had featured so often in her dreams and nightmares. The roses were still there in the middle, but raised vegetable beds now flanked them on either side. Everything looked dead, but glittered in the cold December sunshine. Reassuringly, the hermitage was still in its place to the left side of the building and the covered way to the old stables was just visible to the right, though the rhododendron bushes had gained considerable ground.

She followed the path to the porch, remembering every crack in the paving stones, and took the three steps up to the big oak door with a show of confidence that she didn't feel. The bell had not changed: you still had to yank it and wait for a response from the echoing depths. Eventually, an ancient portress answered, checked her name against a handwritten list and let her in.

As soon as the door was opened and she stepped inside, the pungent smell of furniture polish took her straight back to her twenty-four-year-old self. It was a mixture of beeswax and linseed oil, with a hint of pine turpentine. She remembered studying the ingredients on the tin (there was so little to read) before polishing the Jacobean chest in the hall. It had been placed with great precision under the hall mirror and was still there. Rule number one: don't alter the position of any pieces of furniture.

The door to the refectory was on the left and she had to stop herself knocking before going in. She had a sharp memory of being instructed on the rituals of 'laying up' when it became one of her early morning duties. In retrospect, her mentor had probably had a bad case of OCD, but her manner was harsh and her commands terse. The place settings had to be exactly one scapular's width apart and the water glasses at two o'clock, or it all had to be done again.

Of course, it was no longer the refectory – probably because, as she knew, numbers had greatly declined in the last twenty years. It looked like some kind of community room or art room. There were cupboards lining the walls, which soon revealed orderly piles of sugar paper, pots of poster paint, even glitter and feathers. It was curiously like a playschool. The trestle tables were pushed back to make space and seemed to carry no muscle memory of the hierarchical arrangement they had once known. The lectern had gone as well, the locus of that commanding voice, force-feeding them with deeply dubious instructional texts while they ate in silence. When it stopped, the meal was over, so you had to monitor the rise and fall closely. She had learned to bow and file out in order of seniority, coming in at the tail end for a long time.

The door opened suddenly and some kind of senior figure appeared, judging by her bearing. She introduced herself as Agnes, the Assistant Superior, and nodded rather than shaking hands – possibly because of lingering Covid restrictions, but more likely to express her disapproval of an unsanctioned presence in the art room. Lizzie was relieved to discover that she didn't recognise her. She was young – probably no older than Lizzie herself. Welcoming but cool, her face was stiff. The words of welcome hid a wariness that carried a slight flare of dismissiveness. It was nearly under control, but not quite. Why? What did she know about her? Who was in charge of the narrative of those days?

Assistant Agnes was taking her through the programme of the next four days – the hours of silence, the optional individual sessions, meal times, chapel times, access to the art room – and she had to pull herself back into the present to be sure that she missed nothing. Everything was mapped around the offices in chapel, as she had expected, and she caught herself wondering if the music would be the same; if the Community still had to make the same deep bows as they came in; if they were still strictly summoned by bells, dropping everything as the first note sounded?

She was surprised by the difference the lack of a habit made. It had conferred a degree of dignity and apartness, so its loss was a kind of exposure. There was no wimple – no veil at all, in fact. Without it, the facial expression had to carry much more weight and there was no disguising the lines at the neck. Agnes was wearing a habit of sorts, but it was basically a knee-length, greenish-blue pinafore dress over a cream roll neck. No scapular and no rope girdle round the waist, with the three knots symbolising the vows and the wooden cross hanging from it, but there was still a large silver crucifix, chest height, engraved with the Community motto – *The truth shall set you free.*

The memory of her own 'clothing' flashed in front of her, the way each element was blessed on the altar before it was handed to her: the turquoise habit, the white collar and veil, the rope girdle with its wooden cross… She had been full of idealism – and total self-absorption, probably – but it was a beautiful moment and nobody had made her do it. It was only later that the line from that Shakespearian sonnet had entered her soul – *lilies that fester smell far worse than weeds.*

Agnes was waiting for her assent to the proposed programme and a perceptible impatience was creeping into her controlled demeanour. Lizzie recovered herself quickly and followed her out of the art room and into the chapel.

She was not prepared for the impact of that wash of blue and gold light from the modern stained glass, as it flooded through the simple, barn-like space and lit up the bleached beams and the pitch pine choir stalls. It was beauty that had captured her in the beginning and beauty that had kept her there for six long years. Beauty and simplicity. The haunting beauty of the plainsong had only intensified that. The choir screen was still in place, separating the Community from the visitors, but there were people dotted about – inside the enclosure – who were not wearing the same uniform as Agnes, and they were lounging about, not sitting upright as the Customary had always dictated. Something was very different. She turned enquiringly to Agnes, who answered her unspoken question:

'You will see the enclosure has gone. Guests are allowed in the choir. We are a modern community. Vatican Two has been followed to the letter.'

Something jarred in her clipped tone as she boasted of their progressive response to the papal reforms that had upturned everything, but Lizzie could not yet fathom what it was. It was nearly midday and the bell had gone for one of the daily offices. Agnes excused herself and invited Lizzie to stay and participate. What did she mean by "participate"? If it meant joining them on the other side of the screen, Lizzie was quite clear that she wasn't up for that. She had her own boundary lines.

Agnes sat very upright, with her back to the choir screen, facing towards the altar. The choir stalls faced inwards, eyeballing each other across the space. The altar formed the fourth part of the square, its embroidered purple frontal defining the liturgical season of Advent. No candles lit for this routine midday office. So far so normal, but then the Community members started to arrive – through the door at the altar end.

The body language was all wrong. Where once there would have been deep bows to the reserved sacrament in the wall behind the altar, the 'sisters' ambled in, made a perfunctory bow and sat down without any ceremony, some wearing masks and some not. There used to be a term for the respectful and dignified demeanour expected in chapel. "Recollected" was the word that finally emerged, as Lizzie noticed the marked absence of it in the rumpled and distracted crew that finally assembled. The modern alternative to the habit had left them all stranded – neither fish nor fowl. Without the dignity of the habit, they were just a motley collection of women, who had chosen this rather bizarre profession for their own reasons. All vestiges of heroism had fallen away. Perhaps this was what Vatican Two intended, but it was a kind of carnage for those who remained. She waited to see who the other Superiors would be, remembering that the three of them sat in a row with their backs to the choir screen; the Mother – or whatever she was called now – sitting in the middle. Agnes settled herself at one end; the other end would normally be the seat of the Novice Guardian. Within minutes, she was shocked to observe Magdalen taking that seat. She was still there, after all that had happened. She entered with all the grace and dignity that the others lacked, condemning them to oblivion without a word being said. She was tall and slim, her hair, still dark, was swept up in a clip, and she moved with the balanced gait of the ballet dancer she had once trained to be. She appeared totally recollected, the perfect nun, but Lizzie knew full well that she was completely aware of the power her beauty conferred.

She watched carefully to see if she could pick out Maria, her own beloved Novice Guardian from years ago, when she and Magdalen had shared the same novitiate. Lately, she had become disturbed about her, had begun to dream about her, and needed to know if she was alright. They had not stayed in touch, except at Christmas, but there had always been an unspoken bond between them and she was the only person who would understand what was troubling her now. Lizzie continued to scan the choir stalls for her familiar face, not even knowing if she would have retained the traditional habit, as one or two of the older ones had, but there was nothing there. As the psalms were chanted from side to side, the lesson read and the hymn sung, she began to recognise some of the old faces. Many of them looked strangely absent, as if they were there in body but not in spirit. One of them stood out as the only one whose habit was neat and pressed, who sat upright and sang with care and precision. It was almost as if the others had distanced themselves from her, as if to indicate that they didn't share her enthusiasm.

She was a lot younger than the others, but as she wasn't wearing a white veil, it was hard to tell whether she was a novice, though there were subtle indications, the obvious one being a plain, round-necked t-shirt instead of the roll collar. Her hair was short and springy and dark, her eyes also dark and her skin an olive colour, giving her a Mediterranean look that was both lively and alert. Lizzie felt encouraged by her presence, but couldn't help wondering what made her stand out like that. Did she know something the others didn't or was she just young?

At the end of the brief service, the sisters were dismissed by a nod from Agnes and they all filed out. Lunch was scheduled for 12.30pm, so Lizzie had time to explore a little before being escorted into the new refectory, which she remembered being the Mother's room in her day. Where was the Mother now? Clearly, she would be called something else, but she should have been in chapel for the midday office – between Agnes and Magdalen so where was she?

She wasn't in the refectory either and the meals were manifestly still silent, so she couldn't ask. It wasn't a formal meal and there was no lectern, so they served themselves and brought their plates back to shared round tables, which were socially distanced but still embarrassing in their nose-to-nose intimacy. The superiors were sitting at a separate table by the window and Lizzie felt their gaze on her back, but didn't dare go and speak to them directly. It was as if a force field surrounded them and the inhibition around silence was too strong to break. It would have been like vomiting in public.

It was a powerful image and immediately made her wonder what needed to be expelled so violently. She remembered how shocked she had been at her first silent meal in the Community, which was served in individual wooden bowls. It was baked beans with two rashers of bacon each. There was some stale-looking bread on offer, which she was glad she hadn't accepted when she saw the mould on her neighbour's portion as she diligently mopped up all the sauce. What no one had told her was that this same bowl had to be used for the rice pudding that followed and she had the humiliation of seeing her bowl returned to her with the rice pudding floating in the baked bean juice, garnished with the white bones from the bacon. That was the start of her education in humility. It all came under the vow of poverty. Or was it obedience? Whatever it was, you were meant to learn that the ego had to be vanquished and nothing was yours by right. It was the same about knocking before you entered a room – even your own "cell". And anything you needed – from soap to sanitary towels – had to be publicly requested, at least when you were a novice or a junior.

Having no choice about what you ate and no money to buy things certainly taught you what was necessary for existence, and how to appreciate things for their own selves rather than in order to possess them. You were allowed a pen, but no clothes other than your habit, no books or pictures or music. Real poverty would have produced the same effect, so perhaps it was a perverse choice, but it really bit into your soul – for good or ill. The room was emptying around her and Lizzie hurriedly consulted her programme to make sure she wasn't late for her first scheduled event. She was supposed to meet the Mother, but wondered if it was likely to happen when she was nowhere to be seen. As if by magic, a note appeared on the table beside her plate. Mother would meet her in the summerhouse at 2pm. It was about 1.15pm, so she had time to find her room and discover where the summerhouse was.

She had been told on arrival that her room was St Cecilia's, in the main building, on the first floor by the lift. This meant it was in the Sisters' House, which used to be part of the enclosure and strictly forbidden to visitors. She had to overcome an almost physical inhibition in order to open the door and cross the threshold, from which she had been banished all those years ago. The smell was immediately familiar – again, furniture polish, but this time mixed with rich notes of incense, drifting in from the adjacent chapel. A right turn used to take you to the sacristy where it was her job to cleanse the Communion vessels and lay out the priest's vestments each day when she was chapel novice. She vaguely remembered something about the alpha and omega shape you had to make with the vestments when you laid them out on the vestment cupboard, but couldn't quite remember what you did it with – was it the stole and the girdle or was there something else? The senior sacristan was very fastidious and not patient with clumsy mistakes, particularly in novices new to high church rituals, as she had been.

There was a back way to the chapel from the sacristy, as you would expect, and it had always been her favourite route, as it took you through the Lady Chapel, which had a primitive, bronze sculpture of a mother howling for her children. There was not an ounce of sentimentality in it and it could have been fashioned yesterday in response to the horrors reported daily on the news. Still there, thank God. It was in stark contrast to the simpering statue of the Virgin and Child that stood in the main chapel and was the first thing visitors saw when they came through the old oak door into the nave. She stuck her head round the door and there it was, in all its glory. 'Whose decision was that?' she muttered to herself, as she made her way up the stairs to St Cecilia's.

It was very odd to encounter carpet on the stairs, where once there had been creaking boards and threadbare rugs. She remembered rather wryly the occasion when the Community had bought a terraced house for novitiate accommodation and ripped out a new carpet, replacing it with expensive vinyl, because it felt too indulgent!

Anyway, here she was now, outside her cell/guest room. What would it be like? The immediate difference was that it had an ensuite. There was also a duvet on the bed, where once there were just tight sheets and blankets. There were pictures on the wall, bookshelves, a wardrobe, comfy chair, even a vase with daffodils in. No prayer desk, but that was no surprise.

She unpacked her clothes and hung them up in the wardrobe, putting off further exploration as it was close to 2pm and she knew it would not be acceptable to be late for her "audience". No one had told her who it would be, so she found herself going through the possible candidates as she descended the stairs.

She was no further on when she arrived at the door of the summerhouse – mercifully visible from the main hall. There was a wheelchair being manhandled over the threshold at the other side and she saw with a shock that it was her beloved Maria, her face weathered and aged like an old apple. She turned at that moment and smiled in recognition and welcome. Lizzie found herself in tears immediately, as if she had only left yesterday.

It was clear that she was not OK, as her breathing was too quick and quite shallow, but she put out both her hands with the same instinctive warmth that had always characterised her and they began to talk. She was only twelve years older than Lizzie, but she had aged alarmingly in the years since Lizzie had been her devoted novice. Magdalen, too, had been her novice, the senior novice who had made all their lives a misery. Maria had not been a match for her, as she could never believe that somebody could be so devious and manipulative. It was so hard to get past the Keatsian view that beauty was truth; truth, beauty. Everybody was mesmerised by her, so that she was always believed, even when the evidence was stacked against her.

Even now, she was saying, 'Ask Magdalen,' in response to all Lizzie's questions about the way things were run.

'Come on, you are the Mother!' Lizzie said.

'No, not the Mother, the Leader,' she responded. 'The Chapter changed the name last year, and it was agreed that all decisions had to be made jointly by the three Superiors. They said it was more egalitarian and fairer – to prevent abuses of power.'

'And does it?' Lizzie asked with a smile, only to be faced by a sudden outburst of tears.

'I'm sorry! Take no notice of me. I am just getting old and feeble.'

By Lizzie's calculations, her friend could not be older than her early sixties.

'What is wrong with you?' she said, abruptly. 'Why are you in a wheelchair?'

There was a pause, then she said, hesitatingly, 'I don't really know. I have no energy. I can't concentrate. It feels like I am in a fog. I've tested for Covid lots of times, so I know it's not that.'

'Have you seen a doctor?'

'No. Agnes and Magdalen both said I just needed some time out and they would cover for me.'

'Oh, did they? Why does that not surprise me?!'

She tried to make light of it, but Maria's response was instantly sobering.

'Help me!' she said.

Before she could say more, Agnes appeared at the door and made it clear Maria's presence was required.

Lizzie helped her old friend manoeuvre the wheelchair over the threshold of the summerhouse, trying to convey her support wordlessly, but Agnes took over in a forceful manner, so she went back to her room to think. A doctor would have to be found, but how was she going to make that happen in the current circumstances? She knew she had read too many crime novels, but her head was full of laburnum seeds and small, regular doses of arsenic. It was probably simply chronic fatigue.

CHAPTER TWO

The retreat conductor was meeting them for the first time in the nave after tea, at 4.15pm, giving them a small bite of silence afterwards before they all gathered for Vespers. It was only 3pm, so Lizzie went down the garden stair and headed for the hermitage, where she knew she would find the silence and space she craved.

She lit a candle on the simple altar and sat on the stone bench as dusk gathered outside. She could sense the anxiety in her body as the realisation grew that Maria was not going to be able to help her, and she was going to have to do this journey on her own. Focusing on the flame of the candle helped her reach a quieter place, where she could begin to name what it was she needed from this retreat.

It was to do with the spell that Magdalen had cast over her. She had personified a beautiful vision of total self-giving, which Lizzie had embraced with every fibre of her being. She had felt like an ancient knight dedicating herself in an all-night vigil before setting off on the quest for the holy grail. It was bound to bump up against reality, but it had been in such a brutal way.

She could hardly bear to think about it now. She felt so

naïve and gullible, but she was tormented by the question of whether Magdalen had ever really believed in the vision, or whether it was all a con from the start. Were her six years in the convent a total waste, or was there something there that was authentic and life-giving? Something the others had found and lived out with integrity. Maria would have known the answer. Now she would have to find it for herself. The resolution calmed the unease in her body and she was able to sit in stillness until the flame guttered and died.

By 4.15pm, she was in her seat in the nave, on the end of a row containing the other three retreatants, and was appalled but not surprised to see that it was Magdalen who came in to face them. She was their star, after all, with people coming from across the country to attend her retreats.

It was the first time they had been face to face for at least twenty years and it was not the place to be rehashing their past, with the other retreatants present, so Lizzie simply said, 'Hello, Sister,' and filled in one of the empty time slots for an individual session with her. She could almost see the cogs whirring behind Magdalen's mask of serenity, as she worked out what strategy to adopt. It was quite a pleasant feeling to see her on the back foot for once.

Her theme for the retreat was what had drawn Lizzie to the idea in the first place, when she had seen it advertised online. They had not specified which sister would be running it, though she suspected she would have come anyway.

'We will be looking at inner peace for the next four days together and I hope you will take away what you need,' she began.

That's what she had come for, and she felt its seductive pull, but everything had changed since she had seen Maria and her hackles were raised. There was no way she could just sit there, letting it all wash over her as if nothing was wrong. Fortunately, Magdalen's introduction was brief.

The programme said that there would be a period of silence in the chapel before Vespers, so she sat there, watching the preparations made for the service, rating the novice's attempts to change the altar frontal, light the six tall candles and arrange the markers in the office books for the guests. She was rather good, Lizzie thought. Eight out of ten.

As 5.30pm approached, Lizzie positioned herself as far from the Simpering Statue as she could and in the best vantage point for seeing the Superiors' seats. Vespers was her favourite service, particularly in Advent when the six tall candles provided a bulwark against the dark and the plainsong had a particular melancholy beauty. She opened one of the office books that had been prepared for them and saw the familiar markers in place, plotting a route through the jungle of psalms, responses, hymns and readings. So much of it she knew by heart, as it repeated every year, but it could have all been swept away in the intervening years. A cursory glance revealed that nothing seemed to have changed. Was that Maria's influence? It didn't strike her as typical of Agnes. Nostalgia was not something she was likely to be guilty of, somehow.

She waited for Mother Maria to arrive and take her place between Agnes and Magdalen, curious to know how her wheelchair would be managed, as the three seats were connected, like a settle. To her disappointment, the gap remained and it felt like the pilot light was off as the sisters began chanting the psalms set for the day. Agnes and Magdalen, on the other hand, seemed completely at ease, smiling rather smugly at each other as the service progressed.

After ten minutes of this, it suddenly occurred to Lizzie that now would be the perfect time to seek out Maria and find out what was really going on. She slipped out of the nave, taking care to close the great oak door behind her noiselessly, and took a shortcut up the back stairs beside the sacristy and into the Sisters' House. She knew that she had just enough time to get to Maria's cell and back again if it was where the Mother's cell always used to be – in the corner, next to the Sisters' Library. She arrived there within minutes, but it was clearly no longer in use by the Mother and was some kind of shared sitting room or community room. So where was she?

There was always a strict rule about not entering each other's cells, which even now she found that she couldn't break, but her anxiety drove her to knock on all the available doors and whisper Maria's name. Would Maria answer, even if she got the right one? It was 6pm. The Angelus was sounding. She had five minutes at most before her absence would be discovered.

No answering whisper and no way of knowing which was her cell. She would have to give up – for now, at least. It was a toss-up whether she should race back down again and resume her seat in the nave or look for another plausible location. She opted for the latter and found her way down the garden stair again. She could hear the sisters emerging from Vespers as she cut through the bushes at the side of the house and retreated to the hermitage, a familiar refuge in the old days when things got difficult.

She had her mobile with her, as they had not insisted on confiscating them for the duration of the retreat. An oversight, which she guessed would soon be remedied. Who to phone? Who would have power to intervene? What evidence did she have? Would Maria, as the Mother, be allowed access to a phone? Agnes was sure to have commandeered the landline, but what about a mobile? Had they reached the convent yet? They had reached Africa, but maybe not the Religious Life! In her time, they had not been allowed to read newspapers, so maybe mobiles, and potentially access to social media, carried the same prohibition. She could certainly see the argument for protecting the silence, but just now she needed a way to get to Maria.

She looked around the simple chapel for inspiration. There was the roughly hewn altar with nothing but a single candle on it, benches on two sides against the lime-washed walls and an empty space in the middle, with nothing but a shabby kelim to provide comfort for the knees in the search for inner peace – or an answer, if they were not the same thing.

The hours she had spent there, trying to work out whether she should go or stay. She had made promises. She had willed herself to stay, but it had eroded her sense of self so much that it frequently felt as if she was holding the fragments in her hands, in a desperate effort to keep them together. There was peace in this tiny chapel, but it was always temporary.

Supper was at 7pm and it was formal, so she would have to be on time. Perhaps Maria would be there, in her place at the Superiors' table, and all of this would be a wild goose chase… but she doubted it somehow.

Sitting back on her heels on the thin rug, she was distracted by the pain in her knees and found it hard to focus, but it was clear that she needed more corroboration for her growing suspicion that Maria was under threat. Where could she find it? The novice's alert expression kept flashing into her mind and she decided to go with her instinct that if anything was going on, she would be the one to clock it. It was risky, but what other options did she have?

In the half hour before supper, a novice was likely to be in one of two places – the refectory or the kitchen. It would be hard to justify her own presence in either place, unless she had some kind of dietary request perhaps. As she walked, she formulated a plausible allergy, which could be quickly ruled out if the novice was not there. The refectory was her first shot, as the more likely of the two, but the tables were already laid, in anticipation of the hot food arriving, and there was nobody there. There was a dumb waiter in the kitchenette at the far end of the room, so the main kitchens had to be on the floor below. The layout was very different from her time.

It was 6.50pm so she had to be quick, as the sisters would be lining up outside very soon. As she came back into the hall, there was a likely-looking door to her left, so she turned the handle and was rewarded with stairs down into the kitchen and laundry area.

There was a rather elderly sister directing operations in what must have been a state-of-the art kitchen once, but was now about twenty years out of date. It was very clean and orderly, though, and the novice looked happy enough as she loaded dishes onto the trolley for transfer into the dumb waiter, located within sight of the door Lizzie had entered by. She managed to get her attention with vigorous sign language and she came close enough to hear Lizzie's request for a meeting after supper in the hermitage. Once she understood that it was something urgent concerning Mother Maria, she acquiesced immediately, telling Lizzie that her name was Sarah, and Lizzie fled back upstairs, narrowly avoiding the first sisters gathering in the corridor.

She joined her fellow retreatants as they arrived and the four of them were guided towards the guest table, as they all filed in. They were instructed to remain standing until one of the Superiors gave the signal, and it was no surprise to hear Agnes' commanding voice speaking the brief Latin grace before graciously indicating that they should all sit. Sarah and a junior sister served them with what looked like a chicken casserole and they were then encouraged to serve themselves from the vegetable dishes on each table – using sign language, if required. Still no sign of Maria, so it was just a case of gleaning what she could from observing the key players. The two Superiors were on the other side of the refectory so it was hard to discover much. Her gaze was forced back onto those around her and she became very aware of how uncomfortable it was to be sitting opposite three unknown people who were not used to silent meals. Eye contact was a problem, with two of the three looking wildly around, desperately looking for somewhere safe to rest their eyes. She smiled encouragingly whenever one of them looked in her direction and indicated the reading material thoughtfully provided at the end of the table.

As the meal progressed, she wondered if Agnes would make any announcement about Maria's absence, but clearly information was on a need-to-know basis and nothing was said.

At 7.30pm, Agnes stood up and led the procession out. Two of the guests had not finished their apple crumble, but that was clearly of no consequence and they had to fall into line with everybody else. Lizzie spread her hands in a discreet gesture of solidarity and they filed out. The desire to share their mutual sense of incredulity was almost overwhelming, but she had an appointment to keep and only half an hour before Compline and the descent of the Greater Silence. If Sarah was caught talking then, Lizzie knew she would be at risk of a severe reprimand. She doubted if anything had changed in that direction. More control, rather than less, seemed to be the order of the day.

It was dark, of course, as it was the second week of December, so she used the torch on her phone. Sarah was wearing the familiar hooded black cloak and carrying a small pocket torch when she appeared in the doorway of the hermitage, dead on time. Exact timekeeping was one thing monastic life taught you, if nothing else. She smiled to herself at the thought, as it had been such an uphill struggle for a procrastinator like herself.

They sat next to each other on the stone bench, the light

from the single candle flickering across their faces as the wind caught the flame.

'I was here myself once,' Lizzie said, after a short pause, while she considered where to start.

'Yes, I know,' Sarah replied. 'It was twenty something years ago, wasn't it? You must have known Maria – and Magdalen – and some of the older sisters?'

'Yes, that's why I'm so concerned about Mother Maria.'

'We don't call her 'Mother' anymore, but she is, or was.'

'Who made the decision?'

'It was a vote of the Chapter, but not really… I think it was pushed through to limit her authority. All very democratic on paper, but—'

'When was the religious life ever about democracy?' Lizzie countered. 'Hasn't it always been about obedience and humility?'

'It is certainly still the official line. I think Magdalen embedded it into the new Rule when she put it together about ten years ago. Was she your Novice Guardian as well?' Sarah asked in a tentative voice.

'No. She was very young then – only five years older than me – but she rose very quickly, and when I left the novitiate and took my first vows, she was in charge of the "juniors" as we were called.'

'What was she like?'

'Very beautiful. Very kind. Disciplined. The perfect nun. Until she wasn't.'

'What d'you mean?'

'Something started to change when she got into a position of power. I think she began to be impatient with going through Chapter and having to consult Maria all the time. I know she never really rated Maria, even in the novitiate, and she soon made us juniors see that the professed sisters were blocking the bright new dawn of Vatican Two. We became her acolytes, seduced by her vision of how things should be. She led us out into the wilderness and then abandoned us there, to be eaten by wolves. When we started to flounder and question our own behaviour, and even hers, she denounced us, and sent us off for therapy. It was an abuse of power basically. I can say that now, but at the time I believed it was my fault that I was an emotional wreck.'

'There's a term for that. I think they call it *gaslighting*. How did she do it?'

'She had – probably still has – this incredible ability to make you feel special, but once you were completely in thrall to her, she would shun you because you were too needy. Sometimes you were just desperate to be touched. A hug would have been enough, but, because of obedience, you had no power to ask. She was literally the Voice of God, so it was like being banished from the Garden of Eden. You were the far side of the angels with their flaming swords and you weren't allowed back in. Ironically, it was therapy that saved me, because I was able to name what was happening. Does that make any sense?' She was suddenly embarrassed, realising how extreme it sounded.

'Yes, it does, actually. She tried it on with me, but it didn't work for some reason. I must have an invisible Teflon coating!' she grinned. 'And I have always had Mother Maria – she looked out for me from the start, for some reason.'

'I envy you that. When was she made Mother?'

'Soon after you left, I guess, when Mother Cicely died.'

'Was Agnes already Assistant?'

'Yes.'

'So why not just move up a place?'

'She wasn't liked. And she hadn't been in the Community long.'

'That's right – I only overlapped with her for a few months.'

'They had an election and Maria won hands down. Agnes was not pleased, so things have tightened up a lot since then.'

'And Magdalen?'

'She became the Novice Guardian more or less by default, I think. By then, she and Agnes had become a kind of package deal.'

'Will you be accepted for your life profession?'

'Only if I keep my head down and don't cause trouble.'

'Does that include not asking questions about Maria?'

'Most especially!'

'What do *you* think is going on?'

Sarah stood up and began to pace around the small space, causing the shadows to jump about and cast strange shapes across the walls.

'I know this sounds melodramatic,' she said, twisting her hands together as she spoke, 'but I have a horrible suspicion that they are trying to finish her off. She showed no signs of illness until very recently and now she looks terrible.'

'But why? What would they gain from her death?'

'Power. Power and control. They are welded together, like some invincible machine.'

'But are they really so cynical? What about their own vocations, their vows? The retreats people flock to?' Despite herself, she was shocked.

'I hope I'm wrong, but I am getting increasingly worried. I'm sorry but I'm going to have to leave, as it's nearly time for Compline and I can't be absent.'

Lizzie recovered herself sufficiently to ask when they could next meet and they agreed to reconvene after breakfast the following day, in the same place.

Compline had a way of wrapping up the day and making things feel safe, so she sat in the darkness of the nave, with just the wall candles in their silver sconces providing a bit of light, listening to the sisters chanting the familiar words by heart:

The Lord Almighty grant us a quiet night and a perfect end…

Amen to that, she thought, lulled by the comforting texts that followed, while her mind raced through the possibilities of getting Maria to a doctor. Could she and Sarah kidnap her? A farcical proposition, she knew, but what other options did they have in such a closed system? Could she herself contact a doctor and ask them to visit? What doctor would consider it? On whose authority?

She kept hitting brick walls. At least Sarah would know where Maria's cell was…

CHAPTER THREE

Back in her room in the Sisters' House, all her senses were heightened, as she listened for any strange noises. There was always a possibility that Maria's room was very close to hers, though she knew it was more likely to be in a separate part of the building. She started to get ready for bed and had got as far as her pyjamas and dressing gown when she thought she heard a groan or a moan.

The light in the corridor was very low wattage, so she was in semi-darkness as she opened her door cautiously and began to peer out. As she tiptoed past the line of closed doors, she had an irresistible image of herself creeping about like Jane Eyre, alerted to the noises from the attic. It was like a splash of cold water and she told herself to stop being so melodramatic and go back to bed!

As she lay there, unable to sleep, she reminded herself that this was supposed to be a peaceful retreat and she had already wasted a day of it with overheated accusations of foul play. She promised herself to behave in a more adult fashion the next day and was able to drift off to sleep on that basis.

The next day she slept in, missing Lauds, the first office of the day, and the Eucharist and heading straight to breakfast, which was a self-service affair. She was not surprised to see an austere offering of cereals, boiled eggs and toast, but at least there was real coffee in a tall urn. She was almost the last person there, so she didn't linger, aware that it was already 8.30am and the office of Terce would require Sarah's presence at 9am. How on earth they would get messages to each other without phones was hard to imagine – she could only hope it wouldn't be necessary. Mercifully, Sarah was already there when she arrived.

It was a different place in the daylight and she was brought down to earth by the prosaic reality of Sarah, in her thick, knitted waistcoat, brushing the floor and then digging out the old wax from the candlestick with a penknife, as she watched her from the doorway.

'I'm having second thoughts,' she said baldly as Sarah turned to face her, wiping her hands on the full-length denim apron that covered her habit.

'Why?'

'What if she is just ill and I go blundering in with my accusations?'

'No! Something is definitely not right. She has vanished totally. Nobody is saying anything and we haven't been allowed to see her.'

Lizzie remembered the anguish she had felt as a novice when Maria had not appeared for two days and nobody had told her why. She was like a small child lost. Not least because novices then had only one channel of communication and that was through the novice guardian. *Seen but not heard* was still fully in force.

'What if I can get to see her?'

'How?'

'Go to her room in the Sisters' House?'

'Strictly forbidden!'

'I know to you, but not to me. I can feign ignorance.'

'They won't believe you!'

'They needn't know.'

'I'm not sure. It's very risky,' she said, starting to twist her hands again.

'What have I got to lose? What is the worst they can do to me?' Lizzie answered in a calm tone. 'I came here to try and rid myself of the ghosts that have followed me for twenty years or more. Maybe the most effective way is to meet them head-on!'

'Just be careful,' Sarah answered, pulling her apron over her head and wrapping it up in a bundle before stowing it in a cupboard near the door. 'When is your first retreat address with Magdalen?'

'Straight after Terce at 9.15am, so I need to get into a more receptive frame of mind. Don't worry! Just tell me the name of Maria's cell and I'll do the rest.'

'St. Jude. Patron of lost causes!' she replied, allowing herself a brief grimace before she set off at a semi-run for the sacristy.

No Maria at Terce, so after a brief walk in the garden they were back in the nave, where the four of them gathered in their established seats to await Magdalen.

She made her usual graceful entrance, smiling at each one of them in turn as if they were the most important person in the world and Lizzie could see them succumbing one by one. There was the old hand, Ellen, who had already made it abundantly clear that she was the one to answer any of their questions, and a retired couple who were both academics and, sadly for Ellen, were observing a silent retreat. All three of them turned to Magdalen like sunflowers to the sun, drinking in her every word, while Lizzie was aware of fighting to keep a hold of herself, like a sea creature clinging to a rock as the waves made repeated efforts to wash her off.

Magdalen started with a well-known passage from Isaiah, assuring them that they were all individually known to God, called by him and infinitely precious to him. She made it seem like a love poem, intimate and urgent, assuring them that their task was to believe it and let it in to their innermost hearts.

Fear not, for I have redeemed you,
I have called you by name,
You are mine…

Ironically, the passage went on to say that God would not let them be overwhelmed by the waters that threatened to engulf them or the fires that threatened to consume them because…

You are precious, and honoured in my sight,
And I love you

This was the kind of thing that had made Lizzie weak with longing as a young sister, and she still wasn't sure if Magdalen was seducing them for her own benefit or for God's. She was doing it again now with the other three retreatants and Lizzie could see that it was a kind of enchantment, with a terrible power to it. If it was misused, even unthinkingly, it could do untold damage, as she knew from her own experience. The devastation of being made to feel so special and then discarded without a backwards glance. She had seen it lead to suicide and it was not pretty. It had led to her training as a therapist, in an effort to come to terms with it, but it still haunted her.

She wanted to snap her fingers and break the spell, interrupt the pious words, but she doubted if she would be met with anything other than incomprehension, so she kept quiet, biding her time till she had a chance to locate Maria's cell and see for herself what was going on.

She found St Jude's without much difficulty (the name was written in Gothic script above the lintel) as there was no one in the corridor at that time of day and no one on guard outside the door, to her surprise. But the door was locked! On the inside or the outside, there was no way of knowing, but there had always been an absolute prohibition against locking your cell in their day, so she doubted that Maria would have taken that route.

If she had been locked in, what could that mean? Was she a prisoner? Was she unconscious? Was she dead?! She called Maria's name as loudly as she dared through the thick oak door, but there was no response, so the only option was to try another tack. Could Sarah help?

She knew that all of Sarah's time would be programmed, so it was a case of working out a possible gap. She was likely to be in the kitchens immediately before lunch, so perhaps she could try that route again. She found her way down the stone stairs as before and Sarah was in the same position by the dumb waiter. She signalled to Lizzie to meet her upstairs in the kitchenette, where she would be unloading the lunch. It was a dangerous place to enter unobserved but she managed it, and the two of them had a few minutes as the bread was cut and the ham and salad were laid out on the tables.

'Could there be any legitimate reason for locking Maria's cell door?' Lizzie asked without preamble. 'Either by one of the Superiors or Maria herself?'

'No! Absolutely not! Is that what you found?' She looked shocked, pausing what she was doing to look earnestly at Lizzie.

'Yes, but I can't figure out why they would want to, or need to. Do you seriously think they are planning to harm her? It doesn't make sense to me. What is the pay-off for them? Do they like the Community so much that they want to be in sole charge? If that's true, surely kidnapping or murder are not part of the ethos! And if it's money, there must be a lot of it to justify such an action. Feels to me that the motive must be stronger than that. Something raw. Like revenge. What do you think? How can we find some evidence?'

Sarah was quiet. She had only been part of the Community for two years, during which time she had seen dramatic changes, but there were big parts of the jigsaw missing. 'My instinct is to ask one of the older sisters – Helena, perhaps, as she used to be the Bursar in the old days.'

'Yes, I remember her. She was always rather formidable, tight-lipped and sarcastic, but very good with figures. I think she kept the archives, too. If there was anything to know, she would be the one to ask. But is she still with it? She looks very absent.'

'Just a front, I would say. She can come out with some very sharp observations when the mood takes her.'

'OK. How can we get to speak to her? Do you have any ideas? Has she ever been a friend of Maria, for example?'

'I doubt it. Friends were very much frowned on when she was a young sister. "Particular" friendships were almost like adultery outside.'

'Yes, I remember only too well.'

Lizzie saw her look sharply at her for a second, before she returned to laying out the plates.

'I'll think of a way and tell you after lunch. Meet you in the sacristy.'

Lizzie slid out of the refectory door as unobtrusively as she could and retreated to the chapel, where the midday office (Sext and None combined) was about to start. The other retreatants were sitting in their places, looking very recollected and calm.

For once, she welcomed the silence over lunch, as her mind was full of the possible motivations Magdalen or Agnes might have for getting rid of Maria. What could they have against her that would push them so far? If they just wanted to discredit or demote her, there would be ways of outmanoeuvring her within the law or even the Rule. It must be something more powerful, more primitive – perhaps a scandal of some sort that impacted on Magdalen or Agnes. She needed to know – for her own sake, as well as Maria's.

There might be something in the archives or, more likely, the Chapter Minutes. It was pretty likely that the Bursar was also the Chapter Clerk, with access to the Minutes. Most likely, she actually wrote the Minutes. Probably what gave her such an acid tongue! Lizzie had only been to two Chapter meetings herself as you weren't eligible unless you had taken your life vows and she had only just made it over the line a year before she left. The meetings were not known for their riveting agendas and were actually quite a disappointment after she had waited six years to be part of them, but it mattered to her to be part of the decision-making process.

Were the Minutes part of the public record? Would she be able to look at them or was there an embargo for thirty years like government papers, until recently? In either case, she could not imagine Helena giving her access, so maybe it was a case of finding where they were stored and picking a few locks. The trouble was that she didn't know what she was looking for, so how would she know when she had found it?

Despite her qualms, she was in a hurry to get to the sacristy and tell Sarah her thoughts. She might have some idea of a likely place for storing Chapter Minutes, or thoughts about the advisability of letting Helena into their secret plans.

'No! I don't think we should mention Chapter Minutes to Helena. If she gets a whiff of anything dodgy, she is likely to close up like a clam shell. We just need to get her talking about the old days or something. It should work if we go on about how perfect the sisters were then, polished haloes etc. She won't be able to resist coming in with a sarcastic put-down!'

'Brilliant idea! With any luck, it might give us a time frame of where to look in the Minutes – if we can work out where they might be filed, of course. At least they won't be digital if we go back far enough, so no password problems. Where would you look for confidential files, Sarah?'

'Don't know. And I don't know what we think we're looking for either. Time is passing and I'm getting anxious. I don't like locked doors!' She was beginning to pace again, whacking the walls of the narrow sacristy in frustration.

CHAPTER FOUR

'Sister Helena will be arriving at the community room in the Sisters' House for Recreation in about ten minutes,' Sarah said, as they mounted the back stairs from the sacristy. 'She is always there absolutely on the dot.'

'She would be, but I'm amazed they still call it that!'

'Recreation, you mean? They tried updating it, but the new names never caught on. Most of the sisters are over fifty, several even of retirement age.'

'But they never retire, do they? That was always impressed on us. Even the ancient sisters were rigidly upright in choir, because of some old edict about being alert at all times. I used to wonder if they longed for an armchair.'

'All that has gone, of course. Part of the reforms – when they changed the habit and got rid of "custody of the eyes" and all that stuff. It was a psychological consultant they got in, I think, because of some tragedy.'

Lizzie stopped in her tracks and turned to look at Sarah. 'What kind of tragedy? When was it? It could be something like that we are looking for.'

'I don't know. It was over twenty years ago. Can't have been long after you left.'

'We could start by asking Helena about that.'

'What shall I tell Helena that we want to talk about?'

'Needs to be something that won't arouse her suspicions. She'll recognise me, I'm sure. Perhaps you could say I am writing a book about religious communities and how they have dealt with change.'

'Sounds plausible. If you wait here, I will catch her before she goes in. I know she hates sitting round doing mending or making stuff for the fete. She always says it's like occupational therapy in a lunatic asylum! Not exactly PC, our Helena,' she grinned, with a hint of a Welsh accent in her voice that Lizzie had never spotted before. She realised how little she knew about Novice Sarah and determined to find out more as soon as the opportunity arose.

'I'll sit here,' she said, spotting a chair on the landing, not far from the community room door. It used to be the door to Mother Cicely's cell, of course, and the chair was where you sat when you had been summoned. She remembered the aura of holiness that surrounded it, as if it had some kind of invisible fence keeping them all at a respectful distance. Was it good that all that had been done away with? What did they have in its place? She hoped that Helena would be able to give them some answers. Time was getting short.

Sarah and Helena interrupted her reverie a few minutes later. Helena was as she remembered her – tall and rangy, still with a sardonic expression, but now rather stooped and wrinkled. She had stayed with the old habit and collar, but no veil to disguise her seventy-five years. Lizzie wondered if she thought it had all been worth it, a whole life hidden away in these four walls. Perhaps it suited her. She was clearly an introvert, so maybe the solitary life in community was her life of choice. For Lizzie, it had always been very lonely, but one of her fellow novices had complained that she had no privacy!

The two of them caught up with her as they reached the stairs and Sarah led them down to her domain in the sacristy, where she knew they would not be disturbed, especially during Recreation. Lizzie remembered it as one of the few talking places in the Sisters' house, where young novices would find an excuse to gather, when they were cleaning out candles or sorting out altar frontals in that same long cupboard under the window.

Sarah had a kettle and mugs, even some biscuits, which were clearly a great lure to Helena, who had been brought up on the prohibition against eating and drinking between meals. *Was it no longer the rule?* Lizzie found herself wondering, as Sarah busied herself with the teabags. 'I see you've brought yourself back,' Helena stated in a deadpan sort of way, as she munched on her bourbon biscuit. 'Couldn't stay away?'

The slight Scottish burr placed her somewhere on the west coast, Lizzie thought, *up beyond Oban, perhaps.* She was conscious of buying herself time by passing round the biscuit plate for a second time, as she contemplated her opening gambit.

'You're right! I'm doing my Masters on how religious communities have coped with the changes brought about by Vatican Two.'

'That's a long time ago now.'

'Absolutely, but there still seem to be reverberations resulting from it and it's a fascinating way to study the effect of change in a closed community.'

'Harumph,' she responded. 'And what, may I ask, is your field of study?'

'Psychology,' she said carefully, aware of the disdain it often excited in religious communities, but ready to risk it as they had so little time. 'I gather the Community had some input from a psychologist a couple of decades ago.'

'Yes, after you had gone. There was a disturbing incident.'

Lizzie waited for her to elaborate, but nothing emerged above the crunching of her biscuit, so she had another go:

'I'm surprised! I thought everything was so settled and peaceful…'

'Well, nothing is ever quite what it seems. You should know that, in your line of work.'

Her acerbic tone was just what was required. Lizzie pushed on, looking at Sarah for backup out of the corner of her eye.

'Nothing major, then?'

'Well, it depends what you mean by major,' Helena said, rather huffily.

'I'm assuming it was something personal…'

'Better not to assume anything,' was the terse response. 'Maria had to take time out for upwards of a year and we were never told why. Mother Cicely died during that time and Agnes took over the reins unopposed, though she had only just become the Assistant – had more or less made herself Assistant. A lot of people were not happy. Many thought Maria had been forced out, perhaps even pressured into a breakdown. They wanted an explanation, but Agnes' response was a crackdown on discipline.'

'What happened to the novitiate with Maria gone?'

'Magdalen took over.'

'Why was the psychologist brought in?'

'Because Chapter was refusing to cooperate,' Helena said, with a certain amount of relish.

'Did it work?'

'Well, maybe not in the way Agnes intended!'

'Why? What happened?'

'Maria was brought back and reinstated.' A glimmer of triumph played about her lips, but was quickly extinguished.

'Made novice guardian again?'

'No! Elected Mother.'

'So, how did Agnes react?'

'Curiously pleased. It was almost as if she had engineered it.' For the first time, her face registered a certain puzzlement. A third bourbon was needed to help her digest this difficult fact. 'The thing was, though, that it wasn't the same Maria who came back. It was as if the stuffing had been knocked out of her.'

Helena looked genuinely sad and Sarah put her hand on her arm:

'I know what you mean! I've always felt there was something eating away at her, though I didn't know her before.'

Lizzie saw how sharply Helena withdrew her arm, as if there had been a boundary violation, and the old prohibitions against touch came powerfully to mind.

'I can't comment on the psychological well-being of the Mother, as you well know,' she looked meaningfully at Sarah. 'We are all bound by the vow of obedience.'

Not for the first time, Lizzie found herself thinking about the definition of vulnerable adult in her own safeguarding training. Surely taking the vow of obedience opened you up to a potential abuse of power, as well as tying your hands when it came to calling it out. She could still remember the paralysis she had felt in her own novitiate training when Maria, herself, had made it clear to them that obedience was *supposed* to hurt, because it was about the death of the ego. When, then, did suffering tip over into abuse? And when did you have the right to say enough was enough? In her case, something had just snapped in her time with Magdalen, but she now saw that not as a failure but as a healthy safety valve – something like the bursting of a toxic bubble. She might have been banished for calling out the abuse, but she would have left anyway.

But what did Helena think? She was clearly an intelligent woman. How did she square it for herself? She could go ahead and ask her, ask for her assessment of what she thought was going on now, but it was a risky strategy. What if her reading of obedience meant she would be loyal to the Assistant Superior in the absence of the Mother? Their cover would be blown completely. Instead, she opted for a more general question, more obviously in line with her declared research. 'So, how do you think the Community has coped with the changes at the top? How would you characterise Maria's leadership style?'

'Mother Maria,' she said, sharply, 'has always had a benevolent style, but she is weak. Agnes is her Enforcer, for good or ill.'

Lizzie swallowed her surprise at this overt criticism and went on to ask:

'And Magdalen? What is her style?'

'That is a harder question to answer. There is a peculiar bond between her and Agnes. I am not sure who is the stronger, but Magdalen seems to have a lot of influence over her. I think they have some kind of joint vision for the Community, but they certainly don't share it with Chapter.'

Helena's reference to Chapter brought Lizzie back to their original plan to see the Minutes and she was very tempted to ask her outright if she could examine them, but something stopped her. She simply said, 'I bet those Minutes could tell a tale or two. Have you always been the Chapter Clerk?'

'Oh yes! She who writes the Minutes sets the agenda.' She allowed herself a brief smile before compressing her lips.

Sarah was looking at her watch and clearing her throat rather pointedly. The sacristy clock said 3.15pm and Recreation would be over in a quarter of an hour. It was time to close the interview and find a way of locating the Minutes, despite the fact that they were no nearer to solving the problem. As they thanked Helena and escorted her back up the stairs, Lizzie was thinking obsessively about where would be the obvious place for storing a Chapter archive. She knew that they didn't have a dedicated Chapter House like some communities, so where did the Chapter meet? Sarah would know. 'Where does the Chapter meet, Sarah?'

'In the community room,' she said, absentmindedly, as they made their way down the stairs and out of sight of the emerging sisters. 'Of course! There is a locked cupboard behind the desk where the Mother or Assistant sits.'

'They'll be out in a minute,' Lizzie said. 'We can double back and come at it from the other side once they've gone.'

'We don't have a key,' Sarah pointed out, as they marched up and down outside the garden door, trying to look casual.

'Lock-picking is one of my particular skills,' Lizzie grinned. 'Learned it on one of those murder mystery weekends. They had workshops on all sorts of interesting and useful topics!'

'Respect!' said Sarah, as they found their way back in via the garden stair.

The community room was mercifully empty and Lizzie scrutinised the room for a minute, trying to remember what it was like in the old days when Mother Cicely was in residence. Sarah, on the other hand, went straight for the wall cupboard behind the table, confirming that it was locked and therefore a likely repository of confidential material. Agnes had a bunch of keys at her waist, so it was unlikely that the cupboard keys would be anywhere obvious in the room, though they both checked table drawers and pen pots.

'Nothing for it,' said Lizzie, at last. 'I will have to utilise my safe-breaking skills!' The small, pearl-handled penknife in her jeans pocket proved to be the perfect tool for the job and the door was opened with unseemly speed. There was, indeed, a pile of Minute books, going back at least thirty years, all in the same black board with red binding. They both hesitated before picking them up, as it felt almost like a criminal act. But then they heard sudden footsteps in the corridor and grabbed the books, before running for the door. At the last minute, Lizzie turned and realised they had left the cupboard door unlocked, but they had no way of locking it, so they had no option but to run for it and hope no one would notice. Sarah was well ahead of her, but she herself disappeared round the corner of the corridor seconds before she heard the door handle of the community room being turned. Instinctively heading for the hermitage, she found Sarah there before her and they sat and faced each other, breathing heavily.

'Done it now!' Lizzie said, half-smiling, half-grimacing. 'Who will they suspect, Sarah? Will they realise it's us?'

'Depends what's in those Minutes.'

'Will they realise we're onto them?'

'Well, it depends if we are…' Sarah's expression was suddenly sceptical. 'What are we likely to get from ancient public documents? How are they going to help us save Maria? Is she still even on the premises? *Where is she?*' By the end of her question, she was almost shouting and Lizzie could see that she was getting desperate. Why, she had yet to determine.

'We need to check out these books, while we've still got them,' she said, briskly, encouraging Sarah to pick out the years 1995–2000, which were most likely to be the key ones.

'I'll start with 1998, as it's my birth year,' Sarah said, 'and bound to be significant!'

'We're looking for the minutes preceding the arrival of the psychologist,' Lizzie said, opening the volume before Sarah's. 'Need to see if we can get any information about why they were invited in and who decreed it.'

The writing was very dense and precise, but curiously difficult to decipher, as the consonants were so elongated. It took at least half an hour before either of them could be sure they were in the right area, not helped by the fact that the punctuation was eccentric and there were no proper headings. Both of them were surprised by the handwriting and the layout. It was almost as if it wasn't meant to be read. Not what you would associate with the punctilious Helena.

Eventually, there was a half-stifled shout of triumph from Sarah, who was sitting on the bench under the window, trying to make the most of the fading light.

'I've found the month before!' she said, at last.

'Does it record who pushed the idea of the psychologist?'

'It was Magdalen.'

'I bet she thought they would elect her Mother,' Lizzie heard herself say in a distinctly waspish tone. 'She would think it was obvious.'

'Do you think of her as that much of a narcissist?' Sarah said quickly, her eyes still on the text.

'Yes, I do, actually, though I've never said that out loud before – maybe not even let myself think it…'

'That's interesting because it doesn't look like it. It looks like she and Agnes were working together even then. Magdalen was arguing that they needed help to elect a new leader and suggesting that the obvious candidate was the Assistant Superior, who happened to be Agnes. Agnes was being all self-effacing, but she wasn't disagreeing. They obviously had a plan for world domination!'

'Let me see!' said Lizzie, reaching for the book. 'Does Agnes say anything? No, she doesn't, does she? But Helena does! They need a consensus, so she refuses to cast her vote in favour unless the psychologist is instructed to hold private interviews with all the sisters, as well as the open meetings. Yes! That means that they can tell the truth about Maria and be heard.'

'Always supposing that the psychologist is impartial and does her job,' Sarah added, quietly. 'Agnes might have got to her.'

Lizzie found her professional hackles rising at this. 'She

would be bound by professional ethics! And, besides, we already know the outcome, don't we? Maria gets elected.'

'So that was twenty-three years ago! All my life…'

'Yes. How far do we have to go in the book to get to the election?'

'I think it's about a month further on – January 1999. Maria had been back since Christmas. There's a heading at the top of the page. I've found—'They were both suddenly interrupted by the sound of the bell tolling. It was incredibly loud, as the tower was very close to the hermitage.

'Is it Vespers already?' Lizzie said with a start, looking at her watch in the gloom.

'No, it's really tolling! It's not the office bell. Can you not hear the gaps?'

Silence that dreadful bell! was running through Lizzie's mind like a lit fuse to a bomb and she realised they had their answer to the mystery of Maria's whereabouts.

'Oh, God! What have they done?'

Sarah looked at her in blank horror, then collapsed on the stone floor with the faintest of protests. Lizzie caught her head before it connected with the floor and held her until she came round, weeping as the realisation hit her.

'You really loved her, didn't you?' she said, gently. 'You had better go, as there will be a three-line whip and they will be looking for you. Are you OK to stand? Don't worry about the books. I will return most of them – just keeping the year of your birth!' She tried to smile to lighten the mood, but her mind was racing as she watched Sarah go.

CHAPTER FIVE

It was not Maria, but Helena! It was announced at a very short, said Vespers, by one of the senior sisters whom Lizzie vaguely recognised as the one who had a studio and a kiln in the garden. She seemed like a real human being, acknowledging that it was unexpected and sudden, and asking for prayers. Both Agnes and Magdalen were absent.

Lizzie and the other three retreatants sat in shocked silence and then began to whisper to each other about the possible impact on them. The academic couple expressed the belief that they ought to leave, as the sisters would be in mourning. Ellen immediately demurred, saying that the Community was well known for its funerals and it would all go ahead on well-oiled wheels. She seemed quite unperturbed and rather unattractively self-absorbed, Lizzie thought. She herself couldn't help but feel that it was rather convenient for Helena to have disappeared at this precise moment when she had just begun to talk. She was appalled that such a thought was even going through her mind, but close on that thought was the question of how they could possibly know that Helena had been talking to them. Was Sarah observed with Helena at the door of the community room? Or was her death just an appalling coincidence?

The shortened Vespers was over before the Angelus, so they were all disorientated on hearing the bell again at six. Mercifully, it was not tolling, but went through the usual sequence of rings and Lizzie found herself automatically reciting 'Hail Mary, full of grace…' before she realised what she was doing. It was almost a comfort.

She decided to stay in her seat in the nave so that she would be accessible for Sarah and would also be able to observe the various comings and goings in the chapel, if they decided to receive Helena's body for an overnight vigil before the funeral. Her guess was that Agnes and Magdalen would opt for a rapid funeral to avoid detection, but surely if it was a sudden death, there would have to be a post-mortem, unless, of course, she had a history of heart disease or something. All the same, they would need a death certificate from her doctor. Was anyone checking? What about the Infirmarian, Sister Anna Sophia? She never seemed to appear. Why did she not come to chapel?

It had grown dark and stormy since Vespers and now the great barn-like structure looked even more like a ghostly ship, lifting and falling in the waves as the wall candles flickered. At 6.30pm, somebody switched the side lights on and the familiar features emerged out of the gloom. As her eyes adjusted to the brightness, she saw Sarah walking slowly towards her from the direction of the light switches.

'I'm sorry, I have been forbidden to talk to you,' she muttered, without making eye contact. 'Magdalen's orders.'

She was about to walk away again when Lizzie touched her sleeve and said, 'Maria?'

'No news. Nothing is being said. They've imposed a Greater Silence, so we can't even talk to each other. As a mark of respect to Helena, they claim. But I'm scared of how they'll use it—'She broke off suddenly and scurried away towards the door where the Simpering Statue stood guard. Without looking up, Lizzie felt Magdalen's eyes upon her, the power of her presence was so intense. They locked glances, but she didn't lower her eyes and Magdalen walked away, shutting the door firmly behind Sarah.

Lizzie was left with the dual weight of guilt over Helena's death and responsibility for Maria's rescue. It felt crushing. And now she was alone, without an ally – even worried for Sarah's own safety.

She knew so little about Sarah; nothing really, except her birth year, and even that by accident. She was twenty-three, born the same year as Maria's breakdown, so she must have joined the Community very young, something like twenty-one, if she had been there two years, as she claimed. Were people allowed to enter that young? She didn't think it was allowed anymore. And why was she forbidden to talk to her? Was Magdalen afraid of what Sarah might discover?

Who would know? Her fellow retreatant, Ellen, had probably been around that long. She might know. She was sitting back on her prayer stool, deep in meditation, which Lizzie was loath to interrupt, but she knew supper was approaching, so it would not be such a heinous crime. She tapped her lightly on the shoulder, rapidly sifting through possible openings:

'Ellen, I know you've been before on many earlier occasions; can you tell me what you think is going on?'

Ellen was clearly bursting to display her inside knowledge and her eyes popped open instantly as she said in a penetrating whisper, 'I think they will bring the body in tonight – it's like a mini lying-in-state, where the body is brought in on a bier, the coffin draped in a deep purple pall and the sisters take it in turns to keep vigil all though the night. It's quite spooky in the small hours, but it's really moving actually. I have stayed up myself once or twice.'

Lizzie murmured in acknowledgement and then said, 'Did you know Helena?'

'Not really, but I remember she was a great friend of Maria's, which always surprised me, because they were so different.'

'I wonder what it was that brought them together,' she said, disingenuously, knowing that Ellen would want to tell her.

'I think they were both rebels! You wouldn't think that of Maria, to see her now, but she was once.'

'When did she change?'

'It was way back – when she had that time out. She was never the same after that.'

'What do you think happened?'

Ellen drew her closer and whispered in her ear, 'I think there was a man! And they were forced apart—'

'Who by?!'

'I don't know for sure, but Magdalen had something to do with it. If I didn't know how many admirers she had, I would say she was jealous!'

'And what about Helena? Was she the fly in the ointment when Agnes was pushing to be Mother?'

'Definitely. I think she blocked her election. Stood out for Maria—'

Before Lizzie could probe any further, the bell for supper went and they hurried to get in line.

There were only two of them at their guest table in the refectory and both Agnes and Sarah were missing from their respective tables, so it was a solemn occasion, with Magdalen leading them in a minute's silence before she said the Latin grace. Nothing was said about Maria's continued absence, but nothing had been said from the start, so that was nothing new.Sitting opposite Ellen, Lizzie found herself mulling over her comments about jealousy and the possibility that Magdalen had lost out to Maria over a man. It seemed so unlikely because those were the years when Magdalen was in her pomp and no one could resist her.

And what about Agnes? How did she fit into the picture? She had been a successful accountant apparently, but something had forced her out and she had joined their sister house in America, transferring quite rapidly to the UK. It felt almost medieval. What had forced her out? And what had bonded her to Magdalen? She wasn't beautiful like Magdalen, but she was certainly clever. Were they both implicated in Helena's death? What possible motive could they have?

She had eaten supper without even registering what it was, though there was evidence of rhubarb pie and custard on her plate, so she must have been there in body. She was anxious about both Maria and Sarah and couldn't decide what to do next. Who could she call? What did she have, apart from intuition and coincidence? No concrete evidence. Was she seriously suggesting that Helena's death was not natural causes? That Mother Maria was held prisoner somewhere? It sounded ridiculous.

She went back into the nave and tried to pray. She had never succeeded in meditating – either using a mantra or meditating on a piece of Scripture. The words had always got in the way for her. All she could do was put herself in the presence of God and try to be open to Him or Her. In the early monastic years, she had uncovered a deep sense of aloneness, covered with layers of rage and blame and self-disgust, but she had, at least, discovered the ability to be honest with God and stop trying to be on her best behaviour. On rare occasions, it had felt like sitting in front of a sun-ray lamp, the sense of presence was so strong. Not that often, if she was honest. There were many months when it felt like she was in a furnace that was burning off her flesh in strips. But the monastic rhythm of offices and manual work and hours of silence was also soothing, particularly on those days when it felt like she was falling apart. Something to hang her days on.

So why had it become impossible? It was like falling out of love – waking up one day and realising that the people you loved had feet of clay and the life itself did not have enough to keep you from starving. She had tried to carry on through sheer willpower, but eventually she had ground to a halt. Magdalen had moved on to another novice by then, of course, so life was pretty bleak. There was colour in the rich vestments of the changing liturgical seasons, in the haunting beauty of the plainsong as it reflected the different moods of the Church's year, in the rich loam of the psalms as they repeated them six times a day, but it wasn't enough.Her visits home showed that she had almost lost her voice. She could no longer hold her own in the vociferous conversations that raged when her siblings were all together. It was time to go.And then there was the suicide. She had not found her. It was Maria who had found her – hanging in the doorway of her novice's cell by her own rope girdle, with the wooden cross dangling at the end of it. She had taken off her scapular and veil and folded them carefully on the end of her bed. Her name was Alexandra. They had overlapped in the novitiate by a year, though they were not encouraged to talk. She was half Greek and terribly homesick, with no family to visit her, even on the set days. Lizzie had often heard her crying in the adjoining cell, but they were not allowed to go into each other's cells, so they could only talk at Novitiate Recreation and on guided walks. It was cruel and yet it was sanctioned, even demanded, by the Rule. No particular friendships. Increasingly, she knew it was indefensible, by anyone's standards.

As she began to face up to the growing imperative to leave, she saw Alexandra begin to fall under Magdalen's spell. It was like in a dream where you reach out to someone in slow motion, trying to stop them going over a precipice, but you can't actually move. Magdalen began teaching her the kitchen work and she became her little ewe lamb, gazing up at her adoringly, shadowing her every move. But then, inevitably, it became too much and she was cast off, frozen out. Maria tried to help her get over it, but she was too far gone. It was only a week later that she did it. Maria insisted on preparing her body for burial alone. She called the parents and organised the funeral herself, sitting vigil with the body all night, not allowing anybody else to go near her. Even the Chaplain was barely allowed a role. But after that she fell to pieces and had to take time out. Maria's departure was the last straw. And when it became clear to Lizzie that Agnes was not going to listen to her account of what happened and was, in fact, intent on blaming her, she left, too, though officially she was forced to leave. Magdalen didn't seem to think it was her fault in any way. It was all about her ministering to damaged people, who sadly turned out to be too weak. She and Agnes seemed to thrive on picking up the pieces in the Community – at least until the psychologist arrived. But, for a long time after she left, Lizzie felt compelled to tell the tale – like the Ancient Mariner – to anyone who would listen. Eventually, a long stretch of therapy worked it out of her system and she ended up doing the training herself, but that was another story.

It was all nearly a quarter of a century ago. A husband and a successful counselling practice ago. Yet here she was, back at the scene of the crime. She still felt a visceral need to understand how somebody so beautiful in every way could turn into a monster. She had trusted her, totally bought into her vision of the dedicated life, learned to love the life as she did and even love this new version of herself – and it had all turned into ashes in her hands. Was there any hope of finding the answer here? It seemed increasingly unlikely, but there was still Maria's impassioned 'Help me!' and Sarah's desperate concern for her safety. Perhaps she was being given a chance to make amends, find some kind of redemption…

All the secrecy about Maria, of course, could be explained by the fact that the Community was a closed system with a strict hierarchy. Sarah was not yet a member of the Chapter, so what she was told would be on a strictly need-to-know basis. Maria might be suffering from the beginnings of dementia or anything. What was the right thing to do? She had no idea! She would go to Compline and hope that would furnish her with a brainwave.

CHAPTER SIX

This time, it was Psalm 91 that lodged in her mind:

> *He shall defend thee under his wings, and thou shalt be safe under his feathers...*
> *Thou shalt not be afraid for any terror by night, nor for the arrow that flieth by day...*

Helena came instantly to mind and she determined to stay in the chapel until they brought the body in on its bier. For some reason, she knew that she had to be sure it was Helena, which meant that she had to get the lid off somehow. Sacrilege, of course. And probably impossible, with the sisters keeping vigil right through the night. Maybe someone would nod off...

The service was coming to its end – *Let thy holy angels dwell herein to preserve us in peace, and let thy blessing be ever upon us* – and the choir was emptying.

Once the last sister had left, the main lights were turned on and the scene was transformed into bustling activity. There was a loud creaking noise as the bier was brought in on its wheeled cart, two sisters pulling it and one guiding from behind. It was Agnes at the back, with Magdalen and Sarah at the front. The sister whom she recognised as the artist had silently settled herself in her stall, ready to begin the vigil. Lizzie saw that her head was covered, presumably as a sign of respect. It was one of the old black veils, from before the change to turquoise. Was that written in the rubrics or was it her own instinctive response? Sarah would know, but she couldn't ask her. She was on her own.

It seemed unlikely that the first sister would fall asleep so early, but it seemed politic to wait and see how often they changed. There was probably a rota somewhere but she didn't have access to it, so all she could do was sit and wait. The next obstacle was getting the lid off, a rather ghoulish thought, but she fingered the penknife in her pocket and prayed that Sarah would take her turn at some point, so that she could help her. She had already checked the blind spots in the nave, identifying a lacuna close to the Simpering Statue, where she took up residence for the night. It was 8.45pm.

10pm and one change of sister, but no one she knew – obviously primed with coffee, because no sign of incipient slumber.

11.30pm and she was starting to slide sideways herself, jerking awake suddenly when she heard a stage whisper coming from the choir. Sarah had spotted her feet poking out from under the statue and was gesticulating wildly.

It wasn't clear from her rough sign language what she was trying to convey, but eventually Lizzie realised it was a question – along the lines of "What are you doing here?"

She crept closer and whispered, 'It might not be Helena. I have to get the lid off.'

'No!' she said, in more of a whispered shriek.

Lizzie found herself instinctively looking round for the CCTV, though she knew it was crazy.

'Please! What if it's Maria and they are trying to get rid of the body?'

Sarah went pale, then answered, shakily, 'You don't think?'

'I hope not, but who knows?'

Sarah edged out of her stall and touched the coffin tentatively. 'It'll be nailed down, anyway…' Lizzie tiptoed towards the head of the bier and pulled back the heavy pall. Everything in her recoiled at the thought of levering open a coffin in such a context, not to mention the horror of setting eyes on a dead face, but she had to do it if she was to find out the truth.

'Will you help me?' she asked, quietly, brandishing her penknife. 'Keep watch while I do it?'

'I suppose I'll have to,' Sarah said, eventually, 'though you might make a mess with that penknife!' She smiled weakly, but it was obvious she was right. They had to rely on a rushed job by Agnes and co. Muttering a brief prayer under her breath, Lizzie inserted the blade under the rim of the coffin lid to see how it was secured. It didn't seem to be nailed down. It was more like six wooden plugs fitting tightly into six holes. As she eased it with her knife equally at the six points round the rim, she could feel it start to lift. She took a sharp breath and braced herself, alerting Sarah with a movement of her head.

They stood together at the head of the coffin as the lid came off and both gasped at the face staring up at them. First and foremost, it was not Maria, and Lizzie could sense the relief coming off Sarah. But the face was very bruised. What had they done to Helena? 'We can't let them get away with this!' Lizzie said between gritted teeth, as she and Sarah manhandled the lid back onto the coffin. 'Rest in peace, Helena. We will find out what they did to you.'

'You need to go!' Sarah said, urgently. 'My replacement will be taking over in five minutes.'

'Speak tomorrow!' Lizzie whispered as she made a hasty departure from the choir. 'I will get a message to you.'

Back in her room, she looked at her watch. It was 12.30am. So much had changed in just four hours. If they could do that to Helena at her advanced age, what chance did Maria have?

Suddenly realising how tired she was, she fell into bed with the skimpiest of washes and was asleep in minutes. At 3am, she awoke with a start from a disturbing dream. It was so real that she almost felt as if Agnes was in the room with her and her skin was prickling with panic. Agnes had her up against the wall, with her fingers round her throat, snarling at her, 'She is mine! You are too late!'

There was a knowing look on her face, which was almost more disturbing than the pressure on her windpipe, and she knew that she had to work out what it was telling her, but she didn't want to know. Agnes' face was like someone in a film she knew well and, all of a sudden, she realised it was Mrs Danvers in the old version of *Rebecca*. What did that mean? She was the one who set fire to Manderley, wasn't she? Despite being stupefied by sleep, Lizzie struggled to remember what that mad look on her face had been about… Suddenly, the memory clarified and she knew that Mrs Danvers had been in love with Rebecca and couldn't bear the new Mrs de Winter taking her place.

Could that be the motive for Agnes? Was she in love with Magdalen? Would she do anything to put her where she wanted to be, even if that meant getting rid of the people in her way. Maria? Helena, if she had worked it out?

It had the force of something emerging fully formed from her unconscious and felt strangely plausible, like a crucial piece of a jigsaw clicking into place. She had no evidence, of course, except the looks that she saw passing between them, and she had mostly been watching Magdalen, but somehow she wasn't surprised.

But why the fingers round her throat? Was it simply

that Agnes felt under threat from her questions or was there something more? Something was uncurling inside her that she could no longer push down. Agnes knew how much she had loved Magdalen all those years ago – Magdalen must have told her – and maybe even told her that it was reciprocated, to make her jealous, in that offhand way she had, oblivious of other people's pain. Lizzie almost felt sorry for her.

She was so tired, but there was one last piece of the jigsaw that she had to find before she could let herself sleep again. There was the question of Maria's disappearance and why it was necessary. Why couldn't they just wait until she retired? Nobody was a Superior for life anymore and her health wasn't good – laburnum seeds or not…

CHAPTER SEVEN

Her phone alarm woke her up in time for Lauds, though she almost turned it off automatically. The coffin was unobtrusively waiting in the choir when she reached the chapel and Ellen was there in the nave, looking bright as a bird, with her head cocked back attentively. It only made her more aware of what a struggle she'd always had to get up at 6am and sit through Lauds, the daily Eucharist and her own half hour of silent prayer before there was any chance of breakfast!

It was sleeting outside and still dark, though the light was beginning to come through as they reached the end of the Eucharist. For a moment, at the start of the service, there had been hope of rescue, as there had always been a visiting priest in her time, but she had forgotten that the ordination of women had well and truly happened since then and the Community clearly had their own home-grown version. Lizzie was very surprised to discover that she was the artist from the night before and was almost undone by the warmth of her invitation to them all to come up for Communion. It settled on each one of them like balm when they knelt at the altar rail and Lizzie couldn't help feeling that this was the real thing – empty of ego.

When she got back to her seat, Ellen whispered to her that the retreat programme had been changed and Sister Anastasia (she gestured towards the priest, who was just finishing up at the altar) was hosting an art session at 9.30am instead of Magdalen's usual talk. Lizzie instinctively felt that Anastasia was a potential ally, maybe even someone they could confide in, but she needed to check it out with Sarah first – though how to make contact with her if Magdalen was on her case?

After breakfast, she made a calculated guess and loitered in the vicinity of the sacristy, remembering the inevitable clearing up that fell to the chapel novice after the morning Eucharist. She was rewarded very quickly by Sarah's appearance, pulling on her usual full-length apron unthinkingly and jumping as she saw Lizzie behind the door.

'Has there been any information about Helena's cause of death?' she whispered, rapidly.

'No, but we haven't had the Morning Meeting yet, the one after Terce. I think you used to call it Obediences.'

'It used to be the time for confessing your infringements of the Rule and getting a telling off. It was usually talking for me. You weren't supposed to initiate conversations in the Lesser Silence between breakfast and Terce, but I used to work in the Homeless Shelter we ran then and often you were the only person they had to talk to. I'm afraid I wasn't always sorry.'

Sarah smiled. 'I am sure God would not have minded. Or even Maria, when she was your novice guardian.'

'No, you're right. She tried hard, but her reprimands were never too convincing. I think it was easier for her to forgive my obvious shortcomings than to cope with Magdalen's shining perfection. It was hard living in the shadow cast by that light.'

'It was clearly not a comfortable place to be. Do you have any sense of what was going on then?'

'I don't know for sure, but my lovely therapist helped me

to see that in order to stay that bright and shining, somebody else has to carry your shadow.'

'And that was you?'

'I think so, yes. Like that bit in the Gospels where the evil spirit is cast out and enters the pigs, who then run over the cliff into the sea.'

'Oh! Was it that bad?!'

'I suppose I thought everything was my fault. But I got over it eventually – after a lot of therapy, and then my own training.'

'Mm… I had quite a lot of therapy, too, when I found out I was adopted, but the Community has always felt like a second home to me.'

Lizzie couldn't help but wonder what her adoptive parents were like if such a dysfunctional community as this one fitted that bill, but she swallowed her questions, as Sarah did not seem ready to take it any further.

'Will you get a message to me if anything is said about Helena? We need to know if there could be any legitimate explanation for the bruising.'

Sarah was starting to pack things away and was half out of the door when Lizzie remembered:

'Does the Community still have a Chaplain General, somebody who has the authority to intervene?'

'Yes! There is a Benedictine prior, who comes once a year to address us and conduct individual sessions. He's alright. I would trust him.'

'Can you contact him directly?'

'I'm not sure if novices can, but I don't think it says anything in the rubrics forbidding it. I'd have to have some solid evidence though.'

'I know. We need more. Does anybody ever ask for news of Maria at the Morning Meeting?'

'Nobody has dared so far.'

'Could you?'

'I don't know if I dare,' she said, twisting her hands together in characteristic fashion.

'Sorry! I know it is probably asking too much. If you could just get the name of the Chaplain General, I could ask my husband to do some research through the clergy network.'

'Your husband is a priest?'

'No, but he's an administrator at Church House, half an hour from here, so has access to all the clergy details. He could at least find out the limits of his jurisdiction.'

Talking about her husband and his normal, boring workplace made her suddenly aware of how closed and airless it all was in the Community. She determined to shake off the hothouse fantasies that grew out of the lack of oxygen and try to apply logic.

'Sister Anastasia is doing a session in the art room after Terce, instead of the standard retreat address, so I'll be going to that. I thought she might be an ally. Have you had much contact with her?'

'No, I'm afraid not – I must go or it will be noticed.'

'See you later.'

As Sarah made a hasty exit, Lizzie headed for the nave and tried to quieten her mind in front of the choir screen and its simple driftwood cross. After Terce, they would be in the art room for an hour – she and Ellen, the only other remaining retreatant – and then, hopefully, there would be a bit of time before the funeral. Would it be in the afternoon? There was no sign of any preparations yet.

Terce was rather boring – just as it was twenty-five years ago. Too much psalm 119. It had to be the longest psalm in the book! She used the time to try to recall the names of the sisters in the shadows and count how many had survived from her time. Some of her favourites had clearly died, as there were a lot of new ones she didn't recognise. All told, there were eleven of them, mostly middle-aged or elderly – apart from Sarah, of course – but still largely upright.

There was still a Maria-shaped gap between the two Superiors sitting with their backs to them, but perhaps the Chaplain General might arrive at the eleventh hour with the cavalry. She looked around the nave at the modern Stations of the Cross spaced out around the walls and realised for the first time that they were also carved out of driftwood, carrying the same simplicity and brokenness as the cross, but also the ferocity of the sea winds. She abandoned her office book and walked round to look at them more closely, despite Ellen's look of outrage. Someone had commissioned these in the last twenty-five years, as they weren't there in her time. Was it Anastasia?

At 9.30am, she made her way to the art room with Ellen, still seeing the stiff lines of the old refectory superimposed upon the enticing layout of trestle tables, bright acrylic paints, heaps of feathers, sequins, glitter and dried leaves of all shapes and sizes. A second look revealed plastic boxes of playdough – the sort that sets by itself if you leave it for a few hours, and gets into the fibres of the carpet as well, of course, as she knew from playing with her nieces, though the floor here was reassuringly flagged.

Anastasia was in the middle of all this opulence, smiling in welcome and inviting them to sit wherever they wanted. She was dressed in the standard full-length denim apron and already had a reassuring amount of paint on her fingers. Her springy auburn hair poked out from a blue kerchief that made her look Russian somehow, as well as distinctly arty.

'We have two hours,' she said, 'and I would like us to look at the theme of the retreat from a different perspective. I want you to create two pictures or sculptures – one illustrating how you felt when you came and the other how you hope to feel when you leave. Try to focus on your inner state rather than your outward circumstances, but use whatever materials you like to convey the contours of your inner landscape. I am here to help in any way I can, and you can either work in complete silence or talk things through with me before you start and as you go on. There is water and a sink just through that door and we can always shut the door if you don't want to disturb each other. I am Anastasia, by the way. Can you tell me your names and a little bit about yourself?'

Ellen had obviously come with a plan and gathered her paints and brushes around her on the table by the window. Lizzie knew that she needed help to get started and asked for some input straightaway. As Anastasia shut the door behind her, she said, 'How are you, Lizzie? Mother Maria told me about you and said you had not been back for twenty-five years, so I couldn't help wondering what brought you back and what it was about inner peace that drew you.'

She was very direct, but somehow unthreatening, and her warmth almost reduced Lizzie to tears. She also found the muscles around her neck and shoulders relaxing, though she hadn't realised before how tense they were.

'I am still haunted by some of the things that happened while I was here and don't seem to be able to get past them. Not ideal, as I am a therapist myself. But I have come here rather than consulting a therapist because I can't seem to get through to God anymore. I am still too churned up about it all.'

'What kind of prayer used to work for you?'

'Silent prayer. Contemplative prayer. But all I get now is emptiness. No sense of God at all. It feels as if the way is blocked with big boulders.'

'That's your first picture! Or maybe it would be better to work in clay—'

'You could be right. If I worked in clay, I could maybe dig my way through, but I am not very hopeful somehow. Plastic explosives might help, if you have any!'

They both grinned and Anastasia came back with, 'Prayer only works for me if I'm painting or gardening. I need to be physically doing something. That's why the monastic life is a good fit for me. Everybody thinks it's all about sitting round and praying, but it's the opposite for me. It's the balance of work and prayer and silence. When you get it right, it's like a humming top as it starts to sing.' As she spoke, she was cleaning the brushes and wiping down the sink, but still lifting her eyes to Lizzie, who felt completely in tune with her.

'For some crazy reason, they let painting and sculpting be my work most of the time. Sometimes I do commissions for other monasteries or churches; sometimes I just do stuff here.'

'You did the stations of the cross, didn't you?' Lizzie said, with sudden certainty.

'Yes, it was such a labour of love, because the sea is both home for me and a symbol of freedom. I grew up in North Cornwall, so driftwood is my perfect medium.'

'But how does the art help with your prayer?'

'I don't know whether it's the hand-eye connection that works like a lightning rod or the total concentration and focus, but there are times when I get so completely absorbed that I lose all sense of myself and time becomes meaningless. Not great for getting to services on time, but I think it's the only experience of eternity that I am likely to get!'

'I've occasionally experienced that when I've got a poem right, but I've never connected it with prayer. Maybe I'm not looking for God in the right places.'

'The place to look is everywhere, in my experience. Start with a lump of that playdough and see where it takes you…'

There was a big table along the back wall, just about where

the novices used to sit, so Lizzie sat herself down there with her lump of playdough and tried to let something emerge. Anastasia had a relaxed openness about her that she envied. It felt totally authentic and unforced, but so different from Magdalen and Agnes that it was hard to imagine them interacting at a Chapter Meeting – or anywhere else, for that matter. It made her think again about how Magdalen and Agnes had orchestrated their rise to the top.

The first hour was up very quickly and she realised that she hadn't really been concentrating, so her piece of playdough looked like a wall in a coal mine before the explosive charge had blown a way through. Nothing very illuminating there. She tried to focus on what was needed to blow the way through and let her hands do the work on another piece of playdough. She started with a small hole, but several attempts were wrecked by her instinct to blow up the whole thing. In the end she gave up and acknowledged to herself that what she was actually working on was a means of blowing her way through to Maria. When they came together for the debrief in the last quarter of an hour, she was embarrassed to see that her second "sculpture" was just a scatter of fragments set hard. Ellen, on the other hand, had managed two beautiful and meaningful paintings in acrylics, and was able to take them through what they meant with admirable fluency. Anastasia was kind, but didn't stint from pointing out that Lizzie's lack of concentration was the culprit.

CHAPTER EIGHT

They only had half an hour before midday office, but she decided to risk asking Anastasia for help once Ellen had left. As she cleared up the debris of her own creative efforts and wiped down the table, she said:

'I am worried about Maria. Can you tell me how she is?'

Anastasia looked at her searchingly, clearly weighing up the risks of being open with her. Finally, she said, 'You are right to be worried. She has disappeared and we haven't been told anything, but that in itself is reassuring, as Agnes would have produced some sort of communiqué by now if she were softening us up for a final solution.'

Her honesty shocked Lizzie into silence for a moment, but then she said, 'Does anybody have the power to intervene?'

'Only really the Bishop Visitor.'

'Do you have a safeguarding policy?'

'Are you talking about vulnerable adults? I can give you a surprisingly detailed answer,' she smiled, 'because I have just looked it up online. It's mandatory under *the Religious Communities Regulations 2020* for both children and vulnerable adults, but I guess you are thinking particularly of vulnerable adults – like Maria?'

'Yes,' she said, choosing her words carefully. 'Is there anything that covers the power dynamic imposed by obedience?'

'It's not as clear as the Chair of the Advisory Council requested in his paper of 2018, also online,' she said, with a smile. Taking a notebook out of her habit pocket, she continued, 'He argues there (and I quote) that "the previous narrow definitions of vulnerability had not taken account of the risk of abuse from *individuals who have significant power over them and high community status.*"'

She looked steadily at Lizzie and the silence grew between them, as Lizzie wondered how far her new ally was willing to go. Finally, Lizzie said, 'Do the Regulations give individuals the power to consult the Bishop Visitor directly?'

'Yes,' she replied, smartly. 'It comes under the *Role of Visitor,* Part 3, subsection 27.'

This was not the serene, relaxed artist of twenty minutes ago. 'Have you considered doing it?' Lizzie asked.

'Yes. I am not the daughter of a human rights lawyer for nothing!' She smiled ruefully, but the steel was evident.

'What is our next move then?'

'*Our?*'

'Yes, I am not leaving until we find Maria.'

'OK, then. We need to get through this afternoon's funeral first and then I will put things in motion.'

She looked weary as she spoke, taking off her paint-spattered apron and folding it with a solemn air, as if she might not see it again. 'What will the impact be if you call in the Visitor?'

'It's conceivable that it could cause the collapse of the Community. It depends on how far the rot has spread and who else could possibly take over. On the other hand, if they fight it and come up with a plausible explanation, then it could be my head that rolls.'

It was an appalling thought after her description of the idyllic life she had fashioned for herself. 'I am so sorry,' Lizzie said, quickly, 'I had not given enough thought to the consequences for you.'

'Don't give it a thought,' she said with a strained smile. 'Maria must not become a casualty of this naked power grab. I only hope she is still alive.'

She began to move towards the door, but Lizzie held her back with a hand on her arm. 'Please, one last favour: were you told how Helena died?'

'Yes, it was a massive heart attack. She was in the shower and it was so sudden she hit her face on the screen as she fell. The Infirmarian found her and explained the circumstances so that we wouldn't be shocked when we gathered to see her. Apparently, she had a known heart condition.'

'And you were convinced that it was the truth?'

'Yes. The Infirmarian is solid gold. Incorruptible.'

At that moment, the bell started ringing for the midday office and they both fell silent, as if by magic.

Ellen grinned at her reassuringly as she sat down beside her in the nave. She was trying not to look smug, but barely succeeding. Lizzie found herself wondering what she would say if she had any idea what was going through her neighbour's mind. They only had the Infirmarian's word for it that Helena had suffered a heart attack and that her bruises were from a fall. What if she had been attacked? Lizzie had very little memory of this incorruptible sister. She could be part of a conspiracy. She would know which doctor to call to sign the death certificate. She would have the medical notes to hand... The sisters were still working their way through the interminable Psalm 119, despite the fact that it was now the midday office. Lizzie's mind was all over the place – ricocheting from Helena to Maria and back again, anxious at the thought that Anastasia was on the brink of calling in the Bishop's Office. What hard evidence did they actually have? Surely it had to be possible to find Maria in such a limited space – if she was still alive, of course. She knew all the nooks and crannies from her own time here. Maria was either in her locked cell or she had been spirited away to another part of the building, where she was being guarded like the madwoman in the attic. Jane Eyre, again!

The end of the service interrupted her reveries and suddenly Magdalen was eyeballing them from about a foot away. 'Sister Helena's funeral will take place at 2.30 this afternoon. You are both welcome to observe, but not participate,' she said, sternly, as if the two of them might have to be restrained.

'Thank you, sister,' Ellen said in her most compliant tone, which received a brusque nod as Magdalen turned on her heel and headed for the refectory. Lunch was laid out at 12.30pm and they could go in at their own convenience, as long as they were out by 1.15pm. It was the usual ham, cheese and bread, with salad and fruit, but at least the bread was homemade and the coffee was filter, so she had no complaints. All the same, sitting on her own at a table in the corner, she found herself longing for some homemade soup and the comforts of home and wondering how Hugh would react if he knew what they were planning. Cautiously, she was sure. He would want to know if they had followed all the protocols, which, of course, they hadn't. Furthermore, she was planning to break some more – very soon.

It was a consolation that both Sarah and Anastasia were now with her, and it wasn't just one of her mad schemes, but Hugh had often told her that she should put it all behind her and let it go. The trouble was that she couldn't.

She went back to her room and looked up the 2020 Regulations for Religious Communities on her phone to see what else it said. Anastasia had quoted the key bit and there wasn't much else there to help them. She couldn't help reflecting that the mills of God grind slowly enough in the Church of England without the area in question being as intrinsically unlikely as a kidnapping, or an assault, in a female religious community. Men's religious communities perhaps, after all the scandals, but women's communities, in the Church of England? She could almost see the raised eyebrows and the chuckles of disbelief.

It was Thursday; the weekend was approaching, so it was hugely unlikely that anything would happen before Monday and that could be too late. She had no way of challenging Helena's death but she could at least search for her friend and prevent anything happening to her. Maria's cell was on the first floor of the Sisters' House. There must be a window. If she could get Sarah to shin up a drainpipe or two and look in, then they would know if she was there or they had to look elsewhere. Would Sarah do it? That was the question.

The funeral was scheduled for 2.30pm. There would be a three-line whip, so it was the obvious time to implement an escape plan, but Sarah would have to be there, so that wasn't going to work. She ought to be there herself, if it came to that, out of respect for Helena. But where did that leave the plan? Darkness would be a safer option, but it made the whole attempt a lot riskier. And when she seriously thought what she was planning, it felt like something out of *The Famous Five*. She needed to talk to Hugh, as he had a way of grounding her in reality.

He would be working, but probably from home, as he was only in the office three days a week post-lockdown. It felt quite surreal phoning him from her 'cell' – like Bowie's spaceman phoning ground control from his pod in outer space.

As soon as she heard his voice, she surprised herself by

bursting into tears. His imperturbability drove her mad a lot of the time, but she knew she needed his calm, logical perspective to get the whole picture. They had been married seventeen years, but he had been her sheet anchor from the start, encouraging her to give up her stressful English teaching and do her therapy training, all the while displaying an incredible propensity for domestic tasks like cooking and cleaning, and even washing up. He claimed to find them restful rather than boring or burdensome and attributed this amazing fact to his bleak years in boarding school. After five years or so of feeling guilty, she had accepted his explanations with gratitude and done her best to repay him by doing all the things he disliked, like booking holidays and remembering to buy birthday cards. She did have a few special dishes that she cooked for him and excelled at cleaning the bathroom after her years in the convent, but without him her life was all superstructure and no foundations. All lace curtains and no drawers, as her granny would say!

None of this had a place in the conversation of course. She merely told him that she believed something sinister was happening at the convent and she needed his help. But he had heard her tears, so a superficial explanation was not going to do the business.

'What is it?' he said, gently. Thank goodness he wasn't using his brisk client voice. 'Why are you so upset?'

She could hear him moving from his swivel office chair in front of the computer to his leather armchair by the window and she knew he was ready to listen.

'I'm sorry I haven't phoned before. It has been very full-on and I have been trying to fix it, but everything has moved so fast and now I don't know what to do and time is running out—'

'Slow down a minute! What have you been trying to fix? And why is time running out?'

'Maria is the Mother now and she has disappeared and I think they are trying to kill her.'

'Who are *they*?' he said, carefully.

'Magdalen and Agnes.'

'I know about Magdalen, but who is Agnes?'

'Agnes is the Assistant Superior and Magdalen is now the Novice Guardian, in charge of one novice called Sarah. Sarah has been a real ally, but the other two are in league and are trying to stop her talking to me.'

She knew he would be wary of a phrase like "in league", so she rushed to qualify it: 'They have a kind of stranglehold over the Community. All the channels of communication have been shut down. It's like an autocratic state where they control the media.'

'But it's 2021! What about the Internet? Mobile phones?'

'You don't understand. It's a closed system. There are no mobile phones and no Internet. And no underground movement, because they have all taken a vow of obedience.'

'Except Sarah?'

'Sarah is very young. Only twenty-three and not yet professed.'

'Why is she there?'

'Looking for inner peace, I guess. Like we all are.'

'Perhaps. But why there?'

'I don't really know. She seems very attached to Mother Maria, but I don't know the origins of that. We have been focused on trying to locate Maria. That's why I need your help. I'm worried she might be at risk.'

'At risk?'

'Yes. I think they may try to kill her…'

'But what motive could they possibly have?' He was struggling to keep the incredulity out of his voice.

'I'm not sure. Something like revenge. It's a long story, but it seems to have its roots in a novice's suicide not long after I left, which Maria seems to have blamed herself for, though Magdalen was clearly implicated.'

'Maria was your novice guardian, wasn't she?'

'Yes and I think Magdalen was trying to oust her even then by piling on the pressure. Anyway, it led to a breakdown and time out. And while she was away, Magdalen took over as novice guardian.'

'What about Agnes?'

'She transferred from the American House towards the end of my time and quickly got herself established as the Assistant Superior, with Magdalen's help. So, it was all looking very rosy for the two of them, but then Maria came back…'

'And?'

'She got elected Mother, though it sounds like she was in no fit state to take it on.'

'So, the way was barred for Agnes. But that must have been almost two decades ago. Why is there a crisis now? And if they intend to bump her off, why wait so long?'

'I think they thought she wouldn't last, but she has held on, so they have just tried to neutralise her.'

'But what has changed? Why now?'

'I am very scared that it has something to do with me.'

'Oh, I see.'

'I saw her on my first day. She looked pretty dreadful and was in a wheelchair, but she seemed to be coping and I was allowed a short audience. Then she whispered something to me, as Agnes wheeled her off. It was almost as if she feared the room was bugged.'

'What did she say?'

'"Help me!" And I think Agnes heard.'

'And since then?'

'She has disappeared.' 'No explanations from the top?'

'No. And another sister who was helping me has been found dead. Supposedly a heart attack, though I am not convinced. She didn't seem the type.'

'Is there a type?'

'Well, probably not, but she was too laid-back to have high blood pressure or anything.'

'She might have had furred-up arteries or some congenital heart problem. There are lots of possibilities. How old was she?'

'Getting on for eighty, I suppose. OK, I concede that her death might not have been suspicious, though her face was very bruised…'

'How do you know that?' he said in a startled tone.

'I saw her after she died. Anyway, that's not the issue.' She needed to backtrack or he would find out about the coffin lid.

'It was Tuesday afternoon when I saw Maria and there has been no sign of her since. Nobody seems to know where she is or what's happened, and it's been two full days without any word. Sarah, the novice, has tried to find out, but to no avail. I have spoken to one of the senior sisters, called Anastasia, who is herself so worried that she is thinking of calling in the Bishop Visitor, but I'm scared that that will take too long. I think we need to find her urgently, before it's too late. Help me! Please!'

There was a long silence at the other end while he processed what she had said. He wasn't one for knee-jerk responses, so she did her best to be patient.

Eventually, he said, 'What are you planning? And is Sarah involved?'

She couldn't say that she was planning some midnight reconnaissance involving drainpipes, so she opted for a sanitised version:

'We were thinking of checking out if she is a prisoner in her room or if we need to look elsewhere for her.'

'OK,' he said, cautiously. 'And how do you intend to achieve that?'

'Ladders, perhaps, so that we can peer into her room?'

'And would this be in broad daylight or under cover of darkness?' His tone was very calm and level, as if questioning a soldier on exercises.

'We thought darkness would be safer.'

'Curtains?'

'I know. The other option is when they are all at the funeral this afternoon.'

'So, that would be you? On your own?'

'Yes.'

She waited for his response, knowing she was going to be shot down in flames. But then he said, 'You need somebody with you – to hold the ladder, at least. I am willing to do it, if there is no one else, but have you thought of using your lock-picking talents and approaching from the inside?'

She was so flabbergasted at his response that she almost laughed. 'You believe me then?!'

'Yes, I do. You know what goes on in a closed community better than most. You just about escaped with your life – or, at least, your sanity, so I would trust your judgement.'

She felt as if a boulder had rolled away and she could breathe. She spoke with more confidence as she said, 'We would have to come up with a good story to explain your arrival. Could you be on official business from Church House? Something that requires a conversation with the Mother Superior?'

'I don't think that would work, because they could just say she was ill and offer an audience with the Assistant.'

'Yes and they could also say that a funeral was about to begin and no one was available…'

'OK, let's think. Do they know you are my wife?'

'I don't think so, but it shouldn't be too hard to find out. There aren't that many Fergusons in the diocesan yearbook.'

'True. What if I had some innocuous purpose, like inspecting their library provision?'

'I don't think Agnes would buy it, especially if it let you go unaccompanied into the Sisters' House, where the library is housed.'

'Something else then?'

'The funeral is going to be the response to everything if we do it this afternoon. And I am scared tomorrow will be too late.'

She knew he would hear the rising panic in her voice, but couldn't stop it.

'Let me think,' he said, after a pause. 'I will ring you back in ten.'

CHAPTER NINE

Hugh sat at his desk after the phone call, staring into space while he tried to figure out what to do next. He noticed that his left hand was idly tapping out Chopin's *Funeral March* and smiled to himself, knowing full well that Lizzie would say it was a Freudian slip. When he was at school, he and his friends used to process mournfully into chapel, intoning "Where shall we be in 100 years from now?" behind the masters' backs. Did he seriously think Agnes and Magdalen were contemplating a murder? It seemed surreal in the twenty-first century and yet Lizzie sounded very serious and almost panicky.

He had come to rely on her intuitive sense about people. She was the one who kept in touch with his nephews and nieces and bought the Christmas and birthday presents. Books were her forte because she taught English literature and knew all the latest trends, tuning in effortlessly to what each one would like. But she hadn't always been on an even keel. When he first met her, she had been like a wounded animal, whom he could only approach very cautiously. Gradually, as he left small tokens of his affection in her vicinity, she had begun to venture out and agree to small outings, to the theatre or the coffee bar in the local bookshop.

He discovered quite early on that good coffee was a way to her heart and it had been a throwaway remark about the dearth of coffee in Community, except at festivals, that had suddenly triggered the painful revelations about her relationship with Magdalen. It was clear that she had become paralysed by the conflict between her vow of obedience and her own inner truth that she was being abused by the very person who was a beacon of light to everyone else.

But "abused" was not a term you could throw about lightly these days. It had massive repercussions in the Church, as elsewhere. What was Lizzie actually accusing Magdalen of? It didn't seem to be sexual abuse in her case, more emotional abuse, which was just as destructive, particularly when combined with power. It had probably been a key factor in that novice's suicide as well. But what if there had been sexual abuse with the novice and Maria had known about it? That could have been a reason for silencing her, particularly if she showed signs of revealing all to Lizzie. And Agnes had whisked her away very suddenly as soon as she had whispered, 'Help me'.

He found himself pacing about his study as he pondered what could be done within the law and without exciting suspicion. Lizzie needed him involved, and urgently, but he had to have a coherent plan, because they wouldn't get a second chance. How could he get inside the convent legitimately? Was there a religious equivalent of Habeas Corpus? Maybe there was if it came from the next of kin. Did Maria have any family? He would ask Lizzie. In the meantime, how could he get in there this afternoon without arousing suspicion? A gas leak? A fault on the landline? They might not have gas, of course. And the main telephone line might not be in the Mother's room. It was all a bit tenuous, but he might get past a volunteer answering the door during the funeral, if he looked the part.

He dialled Lizzie's mobile and jumped in straightaway. 'Can you be patient with me for a minute? I have a sort of plan but I need the answers to three questions: Does the Community have a gas supply? Is the entry phone line in Maria's room? And does Maria have any family?'

Lizzie came back with a brisk response, 'In reverse order: I think she has a sister; the main landline is not in Maria's room, but the community room next door; and yes, they have a gas supply.'

Hugh nodded to himself and made some quick calculations. 'What time is it? How long do we have before everything starts?'

'It's 2pm and the sisters are starting to gather in the chapel for a 2.30pm start.'

'I thought I could pose as somebody from the gas board, investigating an urgent leak, if I could mock up a convincing ID card quick enough. Might get past a stand-in at the door while the funeral is on. What d'you think?'

She hesitated at the other end and he could tell she was not convinced – he could almost hear her smiling at his naivety – so he pressed on. 'It's the only thing I can think of that is urgent enough. I could get to you in just over half an hour, if the ID presents no difficulties. My other thought was a variation on Habeas Corpus! If you can contact Maria's sister, I'm sure she has a right to demand news of her and even to insist on seeing her, if she's worried enough. You might have to be the busybody who raises the concern, of course.'

'That's OK. I can bear that, provided I can find her number. The Infirmarian will probably have it, but I'll have to be quick to catch her before she goes into chapel. Better go… When you arrive at the door, say the smell was reported on the First Floor of the Sisters' House by one of the guests. I will be waiting there at the door and will offer to take you up. Should be straightforward as she won't want to leave her post.'

'OK. Good luck with the Infirmarian. See you soon. I will do my best to look the part!'

Luckily, he had one of those workmanlike cotton gilets with lots of pockets and places for pens and tools. He also had several Perspex identity cards in his stationery drawer that could be repurposed if he slid out the old name tag. He chose a square one that looked well-used and then found a template for an ID card on the net, adding the gas board logo and printing it out. Once cut to size, with a false name added and a passport photo from his collection, he was ready to go. Eight minutes and counting! He set off up the motorway.

Careful to park out of sight so that his car would not be visible, he waited until he was sure the funeral would be well underway. The doorkeeper had obviously been told on pain of death to keep out all intruders, but he was able to convince her that there *was* a risk of death, so she let him in, clearly against her better judgement. Lizzie was waiting a few feet away, looking suitably anxious, and explained that it was she who had phoned them, because of the smell in her room. She offered to conduct him upstairs, which was mercifully accepted.

Once out of sight of the door, he put his arms out and they had a brief hug before she conducted him past the refectory and the art room to the door of the Sisters' House. Safely inside, she looked him up and down with something like approval and they both made their way as noiselessly as possible up the wide stone stairs, holding their breath as they passed the window looking down on the nave, where they could hear the solemn words of the funeral service. Lizzie crossed herself instinctively and muttered a little prayer for Helena, while he prayed fervently that they wouldn't be discovered. He followed her up the stairs, clutching his father's old Geiger counter from his time in the nuclear industry, hoping it would pass muster as a gas leak detector.

CHAPTER TEN

'How long have we got?' Hugh asked urgently as they reached the top of the stairs and crossed the landing towards the community room and the Mother's room, next door. Lizzie turned the handle, just to be sure. They would have looked very silly breaking into an unlocked room!

'Maybe forty minutes, if they have a Eucharist, but they might not. I should have checked!' She was angry with herself for such a stupid oversight. 'Time spent in reconnaissance is seldom wasted, as you would say,' she muttered quietly, as he lifted his hands in acknowledgement. But she was the one with the lock-picking skills and he waited beside her as she tried to release the lock, which was proving uncooperative. The longer it took, the more panicky she felt and the sweatier her hand grew, so that it slipped on the penknife, which dropped with a clatter to the bare wooden boards.

They both held their breath but there was no reaction, so she wiped her hand on her jeans and carried on twisting the thin blade. After ten seconds or so, there was a sudden click and the door handle was free to turn. They both hesitated. Lizzie realised she was very afraid of what they might find, but reassured herself that if they *had* killed her, they would have removed the body as it would have started to smell.

They burst in, shoulder to shoulder, and the room was echoingly empty. The bed was unslept in and the bathroom had been cleared of all personal items. Lizzie collapsed into the nearest chair, all the stuffing knocked out of her, and wailed like a child, 'What do we do now? Where have they taken her?'

Hugh squatted beside her and put his hand on her knee. 'We need to look at this rationally, if we can,' he said, gently, searching her face to check he wasn't making things worse. 'Either she's still alive and they are hiding her somewhere else, in which case we have to work out possible hiding places, or they have done their worst and they have a body to dispose of. Either way, they will be on the back foot and very defensive, so, if we make it difficult for them, they are likely to slip up and make mistakes. I suggest we demand to see her on the threat of calling in the police, or at least the Bishop Visitor. Did you manage to get her sister's contact details?'

'Yes. The Infirmarian was very helpful. I managed to catch her at the door of the chapel.'

'What did she say?'

'She said that she had been worried about Maria for a while, as she couldn't account for her weakness, despite lots of tests, and she had been thinking of getting in touch with her sister, Esther, herself, especially in the last week or two.'

'So, was she going to do it?'

'She said so.'

'Do you trust her?'

'I think so. I have it on the best authority that she is reliable. But I don't really know and she may have her own axe to grind.'

Lizzie got up and paced the room, unable to contain her agitation. 'I'm scared it will be too late. And if we start threatening them, they will go to ground and we will never find her.'

'But people don't just disappear in the twenty-first century,' he said, with some exasperation. 'Even in a convent!'

'They'll come up with something plausible. She'll be discovered in some obscure nursing home, where she will have died of unidentified causes, despite everybody's best efforts. Lessons will be learned etc.'

'So, what do we do? What is your instinct?'

She paused and said, as evenly as she could muster, 'The funeral will be over soon, so we need to get out of here quickly and report to the doorkeeper that no gas leak was found. Otherwise, suspicion will be aroused. Then we need to do a systematic search of the grounds. But I have to be in the nave at 4.15pm for the next retreat address or they'll certainly know something is up. Can you start the search? You look suitably camouflaged in your impressive gilet thing.' She patted his arm affectionately, hoping he knew how grateful she was for his willingness to take such a risk and loving the maverick in him that was the other side of his cautious logic. 'I thought I would try and get Sarah to help us, but it depends on how much she is being watched.'

'Of course. Where can we meet up after your retreat address?'

'Can you find the hermitage in the grounds? I will meet you there at 5pm. It will be dark, of course, but there are candles on the table by the altar.'

They headed down the garden stair together to avoid bumping into the funeral party, then split up, so that Lizzie could emerge guilelessly from the direction of the garden. Ellen was already in her seat, ready for the address.

'You missed the funeral,' she commented with the self-satisfied air of one who had been in exactly the right place at the right time.

'Yes, couldn't face it,' she whispered, as she sat down as noiselessly as possible.

At 4.15pm on the dot, Magdalen emerged from the direction of the sacristy. She looked pale but composed, as if she was bearing the weight of the Community's grief with admirable self-discipline and selflessness. Lizzie was nearly fooled, despite everything, but brought herself back to reality by remembering the shock of the empty cell.

As Magdalen began to expatiate on inner peace, the incongruence was too much for Lizzie to swallow and she barely heard the polished phrases as she fought back her agonised questions on Maria's whereabouts. If she revealed too much, she would be putting Maria in danger, and maybe even Hugh, but she couldn't let the moment pass without saying something. For some minutes, she struggled to master herself. Eventually, she was able to look at Magdalen and say quite steadily, 'I would like an opportunity to reflect on this with Mother Maria. Could you arrange a time for us to meet, please?'

She heard Ellen gasp as she watched a flash of hostility cross Magdalen's face before her mask of composure rapidly reasserted itself.

'I'm afraid that's not possible at the moment, as she is recuperating in the infirmary.'

'Recuperating from what?' Lizzie persisted.

'It is not yet clear what the problem is, but the doctors are doing tests.'

'I see.' Lizzie paused, then said in her most disingenuous manner, 'If she is in the infirmary, I could visit her there.'

'She is not receiving visitors,' Magdalen said, with something close to a snarl, enough at least to make Ellen lift her head with a start.

'Oh! Are we allowed to wave from the doorway?' Lizzie persisted, with a smile. 'I would like her to know I was concerned.'

Lizzie half expected a gun to emerge from Magdalen's deep

habit pocket, but the expression in her eyes did the same job. 'Absolutely not!' she said, signalling that the session was over and leaving the chapel without more ado.

'Sorry!' Lizzie said to Ellen. 'One of the reasons I came was to see Maria and she's just disappeared. I am worried about her.'

'I understand, but I wouldn't push it, if I were you. Magdalen didn't seem very pleased.' She picked up her books and went off to sit in a quiet corner of the chapel – far too close to the Simpering Statue in Lizzie's estimation, but she had other things on her mind.

Why had the infirmary never occurred to her? It was the obvious place to hide a body, dead or alive. But would Magdalen get there before her? And where would Hugh be now? She looked at her watch. It was quarter to five. She slipped out of the outer sacristy door into the garden and headed straight for the infirmary. It was pretty dark, so she was able to keep to the shadow of the rhododendrons, as she made her way to the side entrance in the covered way.

Just as she was approaching, the windows of the covered way were suddenly lit up and she saw Magdalen's grim profile as she powered down the short distance to the main entrance. She couldn't risk a confrontation; she was very afraid of what Magdalen might do. For a moment she was paralysed, then decided to follow her down the passage, acutely aware that she had no excuses if she was stopped.

Surprisingly, the security panel on the door had not been activated, so she was able to get in without a problem. There was a small reception area immediately facing her, but no one at the desk, allowing her to follow the sound of voices in her quest for Maria's room. The corridor was lit by dim wall lights, so there was some hope of concealing herself if Magdalen suddenly emerged. She had to know if Maria was alive and safe. Nothing else mattered.

As the voices got louder, she recognised the voice of Anna Sophia, the Infirmarian, who sounded as if she was giving a progress report to Magdalen. She spoke in calm, unflappable tones – just as she had outside the chapel – and Lizzie had a sudden memory of her kindness towards Alexandra when she was so homesick all those years ago.

Suddenly, there were footsteps approaching and Lizzie instinctively jumped inside the nearest door. Luckily for her, it was some kind of pharmacy and she could hide behind a cabinet in the corner. Unluckily for her, Anna Sophia followed very quickly, with Magdalen just behind her, and Lizzie could hear Magdalen pointing out some new medication that she had asked for. She held her breath, aware that they were just the other side of the cabinet from her. Would they smell her hand cream? She well knew that nuns were hypersensitive to even a hint of perfume.

Praying that they would go, she was nonetheless aware of strong resistance in Anna Sophia's response to Magdalen's command. She was powerfully advocating for a different form of medication, but Magdalen was unmoved. What was going on?

Thankfully, their voices were receding and she heard the door closing. Was it safe to come out? It was now five o'clock and she knew Hugh would start to worry, but she couldn't leave without locating Maria's room, if she *was* there, and talking to Anna Sophia if it was possible.

She put her ear to the door and could hear nothing, so slid out as quietly as possible, grateful for her well-worn trainers that no longer squeaked. Creeping down towards what she hoped was Maria's room, she suddenly bumped right into Anna Sophia, who was emerging from the ladies, her eyes red, as if she had been crying. Lizzie's heart lurched and she blurted out, 'What is it? Maria is not dead, is she?'

Anna Sophia stepped back in amazement – or perhaps it was fear. 'Lizzie! What are you doing here?' She looked very anxious, not at all like her usual imperturbable self.

'I'm looking for Maria. Is she here?'

'I'm afraid I can't tell you that,' she said, quietly, instinctively backing away to protect the rooms behind her.

Lizzie pushed forward, calling Maria's name urgently as she looked into room after room. Anna Sophia made feeble efforts to stop her, but her heart was clearly not in it. Finally, there was a whispered response from the penultimate room in the corridor, 'Here! I'm here!'

Lizzie almost ran the last few yards to her door and was rewarded by the sight of her old friend, struggling to lift her head from the pillow to speak to her or warn her. Her warning was too late. The door was shut behind her and Magdalen had her wrist in a tight grip, as she said in a menacing tone, 'I'm afraid I can't let you interfere. We are very near the end. Maria must be left in peace. Anna Sophia will back me up, won't you?' Unfortunately, Magdalen had made the mistake of choosing someone who couldn't lie. She was hovering in the doorway and could do no more than mumble, but Magdalen was undeterred. 'Please see that Lizzie is escorted off the premises!' she said in a commanding tone.

For a brief second, she thought of trying to overpower Magdalen, but knew it was too risky because she was taller and stronger than her. Instead, she did her best to look compliant so that she could get a few minutes alone with Anna Sophia.

As she was frogmarched out of the room, she gestured reassuringly to Maria and hoped she was not too late.

'Wrong medication!' Anna Sophia said between sobs, as they made for the exit. 'She will die if they don't reverse it.'

'You mean, they are killing her?' Lizzie whispered.

'Only technically. It's a sin of omission.' Her face twisted in a wry smile that was full of self-disgust.

'But why aren't you stopping her?'

'She has threatened to reveal something about my mother's past that would ruin her. She would die of shame.'

'Still, this is tantamount to murder.'

'I know and I can't do it anymore. We need an independent doctor. Please! Urgently! I will do my best to slow things down.'

With that, Lizzie was pushed out of the door into the covered way and the door was locked behind her. Where was Hugh? Her phone was still on silent, but it was filled with increasingly desperate messages from him.

CHAPTER ELEVEN

He had been waiting in the hermitage for ten minutes and still no sign of her. She wasn't answering her phone, so presumably she was either in chapel or somewhere else where silence was required. He smiled despite himself at the thought that that didn't narrow down the options much. The next service was Vespers at 5.30pm, so it wasn't that. Something must have happened to prevent her meeting him. Her convent training had made her extremely punctual, so it must be something serious. Where could she be? Nowhere in the grounds, he was sure of that, so what did that leave? It was a cavernous building and he had no idea where to start. Going back over his last conversation with Lizzie, he remembered her mentioning a novice called Sarah. Being at the bottom of the food chain, she was likely to be involved in kitchen work, from what he knew of convent hierarchies. Kitchens were usually in the basement, where it was colder. If he was lucky, she might be there now.

If he went in the back way and retraced his steps up the garden stair, he could then get into the main building through the door in the Sisters' House, thus circumventing the portress on the main door. He met no one and emerged silently into the main building, heading for the refectory and possible kitchens below. He knew how conspicuous he would be among all the nuns and thanked God for his fake ID as he fingered his gas leak detector nervously.

Miraculously, there was a door beside the refectory, with steps leading down. He had his gas leak spiel ready in case he was questioned, but the kitchens were empty except for one young woman. 'Sarah?' he asked, tentatively.

She turned at once and he was so keyed up that he almost laughed with relief. 'Sarah, thank God! I am Hugh, Lizzie's husband. I have been helping Lizzie get into Maria's cell, to see if she is being held prisoner. But the room was empty and now Lizzie has disappeared. She was supposed to meet me at 5pm in the hermitage.'

Sarah looked at him in amazement: 'You agree that she is in danger then? Maria, I mean?'

'Yes. I have been searching the grounds while Lizzie was at the retreat address. We were supposed to meet, but she didn't turn up. I hoped you might know where she was.'

'No! I'm really worried now. The retreat address was with Magdalen, so she'll be involved somehow. Did something kick off? The other retreatant might know. I think she's called Ellen. She'll be in the nave, waiting for Vespers.'

'Let's go and find her,' he said, urgently.

'You go. I have to send the food up first. I'll follow you.'

He ran up the steps two at a time and found his way rapidly to the chapel, sliding in through the heavy oak door and removing his gas board ID as he entered. There was only one person there in mufti, so he approached her as calmly as he could. 'Ellen, I am Hugh, Lizzie's husband. She was supposed to meet me fifteen minutes ago and she hasn't turned up. I wondered if you heard anything at the retreat address that would give me a clue of where she went?'

There was something about her that he instantly distrusted,

something a bit unctuous in the way she responded to him, almost as if she relished the possibility of Lizzie's downfall. 'I'm afraid she provoked Magdalen by insisting on seeing Maria, despite Magdalen's clear insistence that she needed time to recuperate and was not seeing visitors.'

'I see. Did she say where Maria was recuperating?' he asked, in as light a tone as he could muster.

'Oh, yes. In the infirmary, as you would expect. Now, if you will excuse me…' She smiled at him in a deeply patronising way and turned to her office book, ostentatiously distributing the ribbons in the appropriate places.

He was only too happy to escape, but met Sarah at the door into the nave as he was rushing to get out.

'I think she's gone to the infirmary. Where is it? She may be in danger! I must get to her, call the police, contact the Bishop, do *something*! Urgently!'

Sarah grabbed him by the arm and pulled him into the sacristy. 'Hold on! Let's have a think. We can't just go rushing in without knowing what Lizzie has found out. Have you tried phoning her?'

'Of course, but I kept getting unattainable.'

'She'd switched it off then?'

'Well yes, but—"Have you tried again, lately? Maybe she couldn't risk it ringing.'

'OK, but I doubt it will be—' He broke off as his phone started ringing.

'Hello! It's Lizzie. I'm just outside the door into the nave.'

'Thank God you're OK,' he said in a shaky voice. 'We're about ten feet away, in the sacristy.'

He opened the door and she just about fell into his arms. Sarah found it difficult to tell who was the more agitated of the two.

Finally, Lizzie was coherent enough to say, 'She's there. In the infirmary. I saw her. But Anna Sophia says she doesn't have long, unless we can reverse the drugs they're giving her.'

'So, they *are* trying to kill her!' they both said at once. 'Why is Anna Sophia not stopping them?'

'Blackmail, as far as I can work out.'

'I have to go to her!' Sarah said in an anguished tone. 'I can't let her die alone. I haven't come all this way to lose her at the last minute!'

Lizzie and Hugh instinctively turned towards her at the level of pain in her voice. 'What is it, Sarah? What do you mean?'

'She is my mother. The only one I have ever had. I was adopted. Never knew my birth mother. She might even be her. She could be,' she muttered through tears. Lizzie put her arm round her shoulders reassuringly, while Hugh tried to help them all formulate a plan.

'What about making an urgent plea to the Bishop? Get him to come tonight? I am sure I could get him to see the urgency.'

'Too dangerous!' Lizzie said, straightaway. 'If Magdalen is spooked, she might lose it completely. Don't worry,' she said, squeezing Sarah's arm soothingly, 'we won't let it get to that. Can we get Agnes to reason with her, d'you think?'

'Possibly,' Sarah replied, pulling away and answering them both more calmly. 'She is a cooler sort of person, more rational.'

'But we may be too late!' Lizzie suddenly said. 'I've just remembered that Anastasia was contacting the Bishop after the funeral.'

'What time is it?' Sarah responded. 'She may have missed him. It would have been quite late after the funeral.'

'We need to intercept her. She'll be here for Vespers. Which way will she come?'

'She's always last-minute. The art room is only a few feet away, as you know.'

'Right! I'll catch her,' Lizzie said, pulling open the door. 'You two stay here!'

Anastasia was in the act of pulling off her apron and stowing it in the paint cupboard when Lizzie caught her at the door. 'You can't go to the Bishop – it's too risky. Magdalen has her cornered and she's too weak to escape. If we use force, she may do something desperate.'

'I'm sorry, it's too late. I've already called him. He's coming tomorrow morning or, at least, sending a deputy.'

'Oh God! Does Agnes know?'

'Of course. She is the Assistant Superior. He will have had to inform her.'

'Did you warn him that they were probably in cahoots and to be careful what he said?'

'As much as I could. He's quite a formal type. Plays it by the book.'

'Do you know when the Bishop phoned? Has Agnes been over to the infirmary since?'

'He said he was phoning at 5pm, as I knew Agnes would be in her office then. I've been watching her office door and she hasn't emerged since then, and it will be Vespers in a few minutes. She never misses that.'

She paused as Lizzie's words sunk in. 'But why does it matter about the infirmary? Are you saying Mother Maria is there? Have you found her?'

'Yes! But she's in serious danger and if Magdalen finds out that they're sending someone to investigate, she may do something rash. We can't just stand by and let that happen. Come into the sacristy, please! There are three of us there. We are working out what to do.'

'Who is this?' Anastasia asked with a smile, as she squeezed into the sacristy. 'I don't think we have been introduced.'

'Hugh,' he said, holding out his hand. 'Lizzie's husband.

Rapidly being introduced to the underworld of convent life and almost certainly persona non grata at the moment.'

'Anastasia,' she responded. 'Soon to be an ex-persona, I think, after calling in the cavalry.'

'Please!' Sarah said, gruffly. 'Can we just find a way of getting Maria out? You said she might die,' she added, turning to Lizzie.

'Do you know that for sure?' Anastasia asked in a shocked tone.

'According to Anna Sophia, yes.'

'If anyone could save her, it would be Anna Sophia,' Anastasia said, reassuringly.

'Normally, yes. But Magdalen has her over a barrel. Something to do with her mother.'

'OK,' Hugh interjected. 'Do we know what time the Bishop, or whoever, is arriving?'

'First thing tomorrow. 9.30am,' Anastasia replied.

'OK. That means we have to get into the infirmary tonight and neutralise Magdalen, so that she can't finish the job. Will Anna Sophia support us if we manage to find a way in or is she totally under Magdalen's control?'

'I think she will support us,' said Lizzie, carefully, 'but I don't know how much she can do. Things may have gone too far.'

'No!' Sarah stifled an involuntary moan. 'Let me go to her! I can handle Magdalen!'

'I don't doubt that!' said Hugh, looking her up and down with a smile, 'but I don't think that a severe case of GBH will help our cause! We need a plan. Are we sure that Agnes will be at Vespers?'

'Yes,' Anastasia said, firmly. 'She will insist on keeping up appearances at all costs.'

'Right then,' Hugh went on. 'We will need to keep Agnes

busy here after Vespers. Anastasia, can you come up with something contentious and corral her in her office for half an hour or so, so that we have time to get over there? Sarah, I'm afraid it will be noticed if you are not at Vespers, so you will need to wait till it's over before following us. Hopefully we will be able to let you in by then. I will try approaching the front door, claiming to be a concerned relative, as we know Anna Sophia planned to be in touch with Maria's sister. That should divert attention while you, Lizzie, do a recce round the perimeter of the infirmary and see if there's another way in. French windows, perhaps? And check your lock-picking skills are in working order!' He grinned.

As if on cue, the five-minute bell for Vespers began to ring and Sarah and Anastasia made their way to the chapel, careful to come from different directions. Hugh took Lizzie's hand as he moved towards the sacristy door and she smiled to herself at the ease with which he moved into TA officer mode when any kind of crisis presented itself. He was so different from her that it was deeply reassuring. Why it wasn't a source of alienation she had never quite fathomed, but for now she let herself lean back against his certainties.

CHAPTER TWELVE

The two of them lingered in the Lady Chapel, so that they could see without being seen, either by the sisters or Ellen, who was in her usual place in front of the choir screen. It seemed only sensible to check that all was as it should be before they risked leaving. As Anastasia had predicted, Agnes was in position with her back to the choir screen and Magdalen was nowhere to be seen. Knowing what they knew, there was an eerie calm over the proceedings and Hugh struggled to detach himself from the ethereal beauty of the plainsong. It seemed incredible that they were talking about a murder in such a context, but he knew only too well that unstable people under pressure were capable of surprising acts of violence. And when you added power into the mix and isolation, it was like taking the safety catch off a gun.

Agnes was precenting and her voice was disconcertingly clear and pure for someone with such a stern-looking face. She had high cheekbones, which gave her a sharp, unforgiving look, out of synch with the beauty of her voice. They were chanting the psalm set for Thursday at Vespers, which happened to be psalm 139, a psalm that always got under his skin because it was so intimate:

My bones are not hid from thee, though I be made secretly, and fashioned beneath in the earth… and in thy book were all my members written.

He couldn't help but wonder what Agnes was feeling as she sang such affecting words, but then he was pulled up short by a typical outburst from the psalmist a few verses on: *Wilt thou not slay the wicked, O God? Depart from me, ye bloodthirsty men.*

Lizzie must have felt the same jolt because she was pulling at his sleeve and tapping the face of her watch. He caught an anguished look on Sarah's face, too, as they chanted the psalm and hoped that Agnes had not been looking in her direction at that moment. Together, they slipped out silently from the sacristy into the grounds. There was no moon, so the darkness was reassuringly black. The covered way was visible thirty feet away, though the lights were on the emergency setting, so not inviting a visit.

As agreed, they split up and Hugh headed for the entrance while Lizzie crept round the back, in search of some double doors. The door was answered by a strikingly beautiful sister, whom Hugh immediately guessed was Magdalen. She was clearly taken aback by a man appearing at the door at 5.39pm on a December evening, but she appeared ready to listen, as he explained that the Infirmarian had been in touch with his wife, Esther, advising her that her sister Maria was dangerously ill. He had offered to visit her as he was in the area on business.

Magdalen was courteous but apologetic, saying she was sorry that a visit wasn't possible because Maria was not well enough. Hugh persisted (Habeas corpus!), insisting that he could not go back to his wife without seeing her sister. Magdalen was equally insistent that she could not risk upsetting her patient while she was in such a fragile state. Hugh then took another tack, conscious of the fact that he had to allow

Lizzie as much time as possible to get in. 'Could I speak to the Infirmarian then?' he asked.

'I'm afraid not,' she replied. 'She is with her patient, who needs round-the-clock care.'

This was the point at which Hugh admitted defeat, because he could see Lizzie and Anna Sophia approaching from behind Magdalen. 'Well, then, what shall I say to Esther?' he began – never finishing because Anna Sophia slid a big needle into Magdalen's arm and she collapsed on the mat in front of him.

'There was a door at the back,' Lizzie said, smiling with satisfaction. 'It was a dead easy lock!' The three of them manhandled Magdalen into a handy wheelchair and pushed her in front of them to Maria's room at the back. They parked her in a corner and Hugh stood guard, pushing his wife towards the bed. Maria was conscious but weak, doing her best to reach out to her friend in her characteristic way and whispering her thanks. Lizzie hugged her, conscious of the imprint of her bones as she did so, then sat beside her on the bed, so that she could hear her feeble attempts at speech. She was full of anger and pain at the deterioration in her, even in three days.

As she slipped into unconsciousness again, Lizzie turned to Anna Sophia and said, quietly, 'What is it? What does she have?'

'I think it's leukaemia,' she replied in an undertone, 'but the tests came back negative. I asked Magdalen if we could do them again, but she refused. I believe she switched them, though I can't believe anyone would do such a thing.' She sighed in disbelief.

'What makes you so sure?' Lizzie asked.

'I've seen it before – my cousin had it. Look at the dark circles under her eyes and the bruises on her arms. She needs a blood transfusion urgently. It's the only thing that will help now.'

'So, are you saying that Magdalen is consciously denying her the very thing that will save her?'

'Yes.'

'But why? What can she possibly gain from it?'

'Power. Recognition. Her father's respect?'

'Why her father?'

'Do you not know the story? Magdalen was his only child. He brought her up, because her mother died in childbirth. She was an artist, her mother – very beautiful. I don't think her father ever forgave her for causing her mother's death. He sent her away to boarding school, not paying her much attention till she reached her teens and started to become beautiful like her mother. He thought she would become an artist, too, and he could show her off, but she didn't have the talent. And then, when she announced that she was going to join a convent, he wouldn't speak to her, didn't visit her for fourteen years. It was only when she became Novice Guardian and started to do retreats and lectures and become something of a celebrity that he decided she was worth knowing again.'

'But that was at least a decade ago and she had already made it to Novice Guardian. Why try and get rid of Maria now?' she said, stroking her friend's hand apologetically. 'Isn't Agnes the one who would step into her shoes?'

'That's probably what Agnes thinks, but I think it's expedient for Magdalen to have her as her lieutenant. And when Maria is finally dispatched, I think Agnes will find she is not as indispensable as she thinks.'

There was a pause and Hugh suddenly chipped in from the other side of the room. 'Speaking as an outsider, I would have put Agnes down as the ruthless one, who was pulling the strings.'

'That's the power of beauty,' Lizzie said, conscious of the edge to her voice. 'It makes you believe that a beautiful face can only harbour beautiful thoughts, but you have to look beyond the eyes to the experiences that made them. Magdalen, for example. What did her life teach her?'

'Grab what you want, because no one is going to give it to you on a plate, I guess,' Hugh responded in a chastened voice, then suddenly stopped and put his finger to his lips. 'I can hear noises. I think Agnes may have joined the party! And Sarah, too, by the sound of it…'

They all froze, listening hard. A second later, Sarah erupted into the room, flinging herself at Maria and holding her face in her hands with a mixture of tenderness and disbelief. Lizzie moved away to give her space, as Agnes followed, her figure stiff with indignation, her eyes scanning the room like the periscope on a U-boat. Hugh instinctively moved in front of Lizzie as he saw her set expression.

'Where is Magdalen? What have you done with her?' she said in a peremptory tone. Lizzie gestured towards the slumped figure in the wheelchair and Agnes was by her side instantly, checking her pulse and looking up at the Infirmarian with a mixture of rage and panic.

'She will come round in a minute. It was only a tranquiliser,' Anna Sophia said, briskly. 'Nothing like the horrors you two have inflicted on Maria!' It was not clear what had emboldened Anna Sophia, perhaps the unexpected witnesses, but she had suddenly come to the boil. 'If we don't get her to hospital now,' she said, turning away from Agnes and addressing the others, 'she will die! And it will all be your fault!' she said, pointing her finger first at Agnes and then at Magdalen.

'Call 999 now!' Sarah screamed.

'Police or ambulance, or both?' Lizzie asked.

'Let's just do the ambulance for now,' Hugh said, carefully, 'while we work out exactly what has happened here.'

'You have no evidence!' Agnes said in a detached, almost triumphant tone.

CHAPTER THIRTEEN

The ambulance arrived surprisingly quickly, approaching from the back entrance of the convent grounds, so probably not alerting any of the sisters. Anna Sophia went with them, so that she could explain the treatment so far. Agnes made a movement to intervene, but Hugh stopped her with a look. Sarah had attached herself to the stretcher and Maria's hand, and nobody had the heart to peel her off, so she went, too. Lizzie and Hugh were left with a groggy Magdalen and a hostile Agnes, unsure what to do next. Were they dealing with potential murderers or was there some plausible explanation for it all? Lizzie could see that Hugh was beginning to succumb to Magdalen's charm, as she did her best Anna Karenina impression, so she moved to confront her with the Infirmarian's accusation of murder by default. 'Why were you giving Maria the wrong drugs? Did you switch the test results?'

She realised too late that she had given Magdalen all the cards and she could now reply more in sorrow than in anger that Anna Sophia had never liked her and was using this opportunity to frame her, so that she would never become the Leader of the Community.

'What I was doing,' she said, with quiet dignity, 'was easing her last hours, so that she would not die in unbearable pain.'

'But what about treating her illness?' Lizzie replied, her harsh tones cutting through the saccharine performance in front of them.

'We had no clear evidence of what it was. And no, I did not switch the test results. She was – is – my beloved sister!'

Agnes was watching quietly, her facial expression slowly melding into a look of wounded innocence and incipient outrage. Lizzie knew instinctively that it was a performance for Hugh's benefit, with the aim of getting him out of the convent buildings and back into his own sphere. She couldn't help wondering what would happen to her once they succeeded in that ploy. Would she be escorted off the premises, asked to leave politely on some trumped-up pretext, or what? She certainly couldn't see the retreat continuing – even if Ellen had proved she could cope with almost anything that was thrown at her.

But it was also clear that reality was about to invade the bubble that Magdalen and Agnes had created. Some time tonight they would get word about Maria. And 9.30am tomorrow, the Bishop Visitor, or someone official, would arrive. The two of them needed to be a party to both these events, but what power did they have to enforce their continuing presence if they were not there to guard against a murder, particularly a disputed murder?

It was still early, only 7.30pm, and they were all hungry, so she decided to try and buy some time by suggesting they have food sent over while they waited to hear from the hospital. At least that way they might be around when news came through on the infirmary phone. For her own reasons, no doubt, Agnes acceded to this request and offered to go and fetch some.

This left the two of them alone with Magdalen. As Lizzie struggled with what she wanted to say to her, out of all the questions she had harboured for so long, Hugh cut in and asked, 'Why do you think Anna Sophia was so intent on framing you, as you put it? Why did she not want you to be in charge?'

Magdalen turned the full force of her mesmerising beauty upon him and Lizzie had to stop herself from leaping between them and breaking up the intensity of her gaze, before he was turned to stone.

In fact, Hugh was perfectly able to ward off her Medusa-like gaze without Lizzie's help and seemed completely immune to her power when it came to it. Lizzie watched closely as he persisted with his polite enquiry, amazed by another example of the profound difference between two people who were otherwise so attuned. She thanked God for him, more sincerely than ever before, though she had had cause on many occasions.

The silence deepened as they both waited for Magdalen's answer. Finally, she said, 'If I'm honest, I think she was jealous. She would have liked to be the Leader herself, but she just didn't have the personality – or the looks, I'm afraid.'

Lizzie gasped that she could have got it so wrong and was ascribing such a superficial motive to a woman of Anna Sophia's calibre. Was she such a narcissist that it really was all about her and other people only existed in relation to her, to serve her ends? Her eyes were fixed on this woman she had once loved, while inside her head she had the sensation of kaleidoscopic images cascading into a succession of new patterns, as she tried to make sense of her own traumatic memories.

Hugh's tone remained even and calm, as he pushed further with his forensic enquiries. *He is trying to lull her into a false sense of security*, she thought, *to see if she will give herself away.* She looked at her husband with new eyes, having never seen him operating in this mode before. What was the word Sarah had used? Respect!

'What will you do with Anna Sophia when she comes back?' he asked as one professional to another, implying that he understood she would have to be dealt with.

'She will have to be silenced,' she replied without hesitation. 'Cannot be allowed to spread such rumours around.'

'And how will you silence her?' he asked innocently, as you would if you were talking about a change of diet.

'She will have to be confined to a room in the infirmary, I imagine. Probably sedated, as she did assault me with an intent to harm. I won't pursue charges, of course. That would not be appropriate.'

'Of course,' he said, nodding sagely. 'And will you have to consult the Bishop Visitor on this or do you have the power within your own constitution? Safeguarding rules and all that?'

'Stop there!' Lizzie was signalling to him with her eyes, as she saw Magdalen's expression change at the mention of *safeguarding*.

'We have a policy in place, of course,' Magdalen replied, smartly, 'but I don't think that will be necessary.'

She doesn't know that the Bishop is coming tomorrow, Lizzie thought. *Agnes has not had a chance to tell her.* At that very moment, Agnes returned with a tray of sandwiches and put them out on the side table with a pile of paper napkins. As they all got up to choose what they wanted, Lizzie was frantically thinking how they could stop her finding out and preparing her defence. Clearly, they couldn't leave Agnes alone with her. Perhaps the best stratagem was to tell her a sanitised version of the truth and buy themselves some time to tell the Bishop of their real suspicions. She looked directly at Magdalen and said in her most disingenuously helpful tone,

'I don't know if Agnes has told you yet, but someone is coming from the Bishop's Office tomorrow morning, in response to an urgent request from Anastasia.'

She watched as Magdalen's eyes snapped round and fixed on Agnes accusingly, as Agnes coloured and instinctively stepped back.

'What is she talking about?' Magdalen asked in an icy tone to her erstwhile friend.

Before Agnes could answer, Lizzie intervened, hoping she could lie convincingly.

'Hugh was in the Bishop's Office when the call came through from Anastasia, which is how I know. He came here to see me and check if everything was OK.'

'I still don't know why Anastasia was in touch with the Bishop Visitor without my permission,' Magdalen persisted, looking at Agnes.

'The call come through just before Vespers, so I couldn't let you know,' she said, defensively. 'Anastasia was concerned about the disappearance of Maria and the fact that they weren't being told anything.'

'Oh, is that all?' she said, visibly relaxing. 'Let him come. We can answer his queries. Anastasia won't be a problem.'

A fine example of narcissistic hubris, Lizzie thought to herself.

'Shall I go home then?' Hugh asked, looking at Lizzie out of the corner of his eye and picking up her tacit agreement. 'I will be accompanying the Bishop, or whoever he sends, so will see you all at 9.30am in any case.'

Lizzie held her breath, as they swallowed his fabrication without difficulty. 'Take care!' he whispered, as he gave her a quick kiss in farewell.

And then, there were three.

CHAPTER FOURTEEN

'Could I just stay until we hear from the hospital?' Lizzie asked, suddenly full of trepidation, but desperate to hear about Maria. They were all in the lobby after seeing Hugh out and she instinctively chose a chair with the wall at its back and a good view of the exit.

She realised that she had never been alone with the two of them in anything but a formal setting and had absolutely no idea how they would all manage a wait that could stretch out for hours. It felt like sitting with someone who was holding a dangerously unstable bomb in their lap. The slightest sudden movement could set it off. And she didn't know which of them it was who held the bomb.

Magdalen was sitting opposite her in an armchair on the other side of the coffee table. She was rubbing her arm where the needle must have gone in.

'It's sore,' she said, accusingly. 'Why would Anna Sophia attack me like that?'

'Perhaps she thought you were going to let Maria die,' Lizzie answered in a level tone, masking her outrage as much as she could, knowing she had to pace herself.

'But why would she think that of me?' she persisted in

a wounded tone, putting on her most innocent face and expecting the capitulation she normally received.

'I heard you in the pharmacy room,' Lizzie said. 'I know she was trying to stop you giving Maria that last drug.'

'Is that what you think you heard?' she countered, rapidly adjusting her facial expression. 'I think you misunderstood. I was just trying to give her the painkillers she needed—"To ease her pain in her last hours!' Agnes chimed in, triumphantly.

'Yes! Just so.'

'I imagine you were both desperately worried,' Lizzie persisted, struck by the marked absence of anxiety on both their faces.

'Yes, terribly,' Agnes answered, watching Magdalen's expression intently, checking she was taking the right line, recalibrating where necessary. Lizzie was again reminded of the volatility of a bomb, but knew this was the only chance she had to get to the truth. Under cover of searching for a tissue in her handbag, she put her phone on record, trusting that Magdalen would be unaware of such modern stratagems.

'How long do you think we will have to wait before we hear anything?' Lizzie said, after an uneasy pause. She had never been good at sitting in silence when things were going on under the surface. It had been the hardest thing to overcome in her therapy training, but now she was grateful for the work she had put in, and could match the two of them, minute for minute.

'It won't be long,' Agnes blurted out when Magdalen remained stolidly uncommunicative. 'The drugs we gave her will—'I don't think Lizzie needs to know the details!' Magdalen cut through unceremoniously. 'The disease will take its course.'

'And what was your diagnosis?' Lizzie asked.

'Probably leukaemia, as Anna Sophia said, but the blood tests were inconclusive.'

'And why no second opinion?'

'She was a very private person, wasn't she?' Agnes said in a deferential tone. 'She didn't want anyone coming in and possibly carrying her off to hospital.'

'In that case, I have to ask why she said "Help me!" when I met her in the summerhouse two days ago. You heard her, didn't you Agnes, that's why you whisked her away?'

Agnes was beginning to bluster and was silenced in peremptory fashion by Magdalen, who said in the kind of tone usually accompanied by thumbscrews, 'You were always a nuisance, Lizzie, always asking too many questions and getting in the way. That's why you had to be got rid of last time and this is no different. When Anna Sophia comes back, with Sarah, and tells us that Maria has died from natural causes, you will have no evidence to the contrary and we would like you to leave forthwith.'

She stood up and loomed over Lizzie, who also stood up and looked her in the eye. 'I will not be leaving until the Bishop has completed his investigation, or whatever he calls it, and we have some answers about what has gone on here. If you try to stop me, I am afraid I will feel obliged to reveal all to the authorities. I owe it to Maria – and to Sarah, if it comes to that. This was once a place where integrity mattered.'

Realising that she had blown it, but feeling somehow liberated of the weight she had carried around for so long, Lizzie sat down again and feigned calm, picking up one of the brochures that lay scattered around.

As if on cue, the desk phone rang. 'We are on our way back,' Anna Sophia said. 'You had better prepare for another funeral.'

CHAPTER FIFTEEN

A heavy silence descended at the news, all of them caught up in their own thoughts. Lizzie was determined not to let the other two see the extent of her grief, fearing it would give them power over her. Instead, she said, 'Shall I make a cup of tea? I think we could all do with one.'

There was no response from either of them. Magdalen immediately went off in the direction of the pharmacy and Agnes began phoning through to the main building to alert them to the news. The two of them functioned as the team that they were, without the need to confer, and Lizzie felt how easily the system could close over their heads and obliterate all evidence of foul play – if that was what it was. She followed Magdalen to the pharmacy, worried that she might try to remove any incriminating evidence, but unsure what she could do to stop her if that was the case.

'Why are you following me?' Magdalen turned accusingly, her hands shuffling some papers on the counter under the pills cabinet. 'This area is out of bounds.'

'I'm just a bit worried you might be falsifying evidence,' she replied, in what she knew was a provocative manner. 'Or at least contaminating it. I think it might be a good idea to lock this door, until we can clear things up, don't you?' She held the door open as she spoke, though she half expected Magdalen to laugh in her face or even slap her. Surprisingly, she complied, which made Lizzie suspect that she had already covered her tracks.

She was locking the pharmacy door and wondering where the key could be safely kept when she heard a commotion at the main entrance and realised that Anna Sophia and Sarah were back.

She could tell at a glance that Anna Sophia was simmering with suppressed rage and maybe something else, while Sarah appeared heartbroken. She put her arm round Sarah and led her to a chair. 'The kettle's boiled,' she said, reassuringly, and put a mug down on the table beside her. 'Do you want to talk?' she said, after a few minutes.

Sarah nodded, though she struggled to form any coherent words through her tears. Finally, she said, 'It took me five years to trace her. There was a direct route, a government register, but you both have to be willing and I didn't want her to know I was looking for her until I was sure I wanted to be found…'

'I am sorry, Sarah, but I don't know what you are saying,' Lizzie said, gently, passing over a tissue out of instinct.

'Oh, it was too late! I don't think she could hear me. I should have told her sooner.'

'What should you have told her? I don't understand.'

'She *could* hear you,' Anna Sophia intervened. 'She was sinking into a coma, but I believe hearing is the last sense to go. I saw her squeeze your hand when you told her. And she did die with a strangely beautiful expression on her face, like something had been resolved, or she had come home.'

'Do you really think so?' Sarah said through sobs, wringing her hands so violently that they looked red and chapped.

'You are saying that Maria was your birth mother?' Lizzie

said at last. 'When? How?' It was Lizzie's turn to feel as if her whole world had been upended.

It was Anna Sophia who answered her, 'Yes, I know it's weird, but it all fits. Maria had a year out after that breakdown and she was never the same after she came back. We all thought she was still depressed, but it was more like she was lost, or maybe it was not she who was lost…'

'I want to be certain. I want to do a DNA test,' Sarah said in an urgent tone.

'But what about Maria? Is it ethical on a dead body?' Lizzie replied.

'She had put herself on the adoption contact register, so she wanted to be found.'

'You got that far? Did you put yourself on?' 'No. Like I said, I wasn't sure I wanted to be found, but now I am.'

'Do they have DNA details on the register?'

'I don't know!' she almost wailed. 'It can't be too late.'

'I'm sorry, Sarah, but all this is speculation, wishful thinking. What you need is to say goodbye to Mother Maria and get back into the normal rhythm of novitiate life.'

'But—' 'That is not a suggestion, Sarah. You are under obedience. As your Novice Guardian, I am telling you that you need to get back to your duties as chapel novice and regular attendance at the offices.'

'And who will help her with her grief?' Anna Sophia intervened. 'You?!'

'God will provide,' Magdalen said, with her best pious expression.

'I don't think so,' Anna Sophia muttered under her breath to Lizzie. 'He might need some human assistance.'

Lizzie wasn't sure if Agnes had heard Anna Sophia's muttered comment, but she suddenly sprang into action with a characteristically authoritative pronouncement. Casting a quick glance at Magdalen, she said, 'We are agreed, I think, that the Bishop Visitor, or his representative, will be here tomorrow, so we should all gather here at 9.30am to give him the information he needs. Sarah, you will not be required.' Batting away Sarah's tearful objections, she continued, 'The funeral is likely to be delayed to wait for a post-mortem, but once that is over, we will give Maria the grand funeral befitting a Mother of this great community.'

Smiling benevolently around the group, Agnes clearly thought that this would suffice, but only Magdalen looked satisfied. Anna Sophia had moved to Sarah's side and was whispering something for her ears only. Magdalen saw this and pulled her away roughly. 'Sarah, please leave now and take a late morning. You are excused your chapel duties tomorrow. We will see you at breakfast. After that, please use the day for prayer and reflection and observe a silent retreat.'

For the first time since she had left, Lizzie could see the naked power in the vow of obedience. It could be described as the benign process of religious formation, but what comeback did Sarah have if there was an abuse of power? There was no appeals procedure. No independent authority to hear her case – except perhaps the Bishop Visitor, but how many novices knew about that? She thought of her time with Maria and the benevolent dictatorship she had willingly submitted to, how much she had learned from the stripping away of her usual supports and the relinquishing of her compulsion to have the last word. But Maria was a woman you could love and respect, someone who had been there before you and not flinched. It even struck her how strangely helpful the novitiate training had been in her preparation for the therapy diploma.

But this was now and Sarah was about to be incarcerated. And there was nothing Lizzie could do to release her, as long as she chose to submit.

Sarah left first and Lizzie prepared to follow, openly handing over the pharmacy key to Anna Sophia, whose cell was in the infirmary building.

Magdalen noticed, as she had been meant to, and questioned whether it should be kept somewhere neutral, like the cupboard in the community room, but Anna Sophia overruled her, insisting that she had other patients in the infirmary, for whom access to the pharmacy was needed. Lizzie had no doubt that Magdalen would find a way in, but, at least for tonight, the key would be safe and she knew she was too tired to take it any further.

Back in her room in the Sisters' House, she played back the recording on her phone and was not all that surprised to discover that there was nothing incriminating enough to provide conclusive evidence when the Bishop arrived. All they had was Agnes' comment that *they wouldn't have to wait long, because the drugs they had given Maria would…* This was followed by Magdalen's dogmatic comment that Maria would be dead from natural causes within hours and there would be no evidence to prove otherwise. Again, it wouldn't be enough. She could almost hear the Bishop's incredulity, particularly when accompanied by Magdalen's charm offensive. So, what to do?

She tapped in Hugh's number. 'I'm afraid Maria died this evening. They're saying it was leukaemia, but nothing yet on whether her death was hastened or whether it could have been prevented.'

'I'm so sorry,' he said immediately. 'I know how much she meant to you. Are you OK?'

'Yes, I'm alright, though I do feel quite shaky. It's all been so quick. Anna Sophia came back looking more angry than I have ever seen her and Sarah was in pieces. There's more to say about her, but the urgent business concerns tomorrow.

Magdalen and Agnes are going to brazen it out. They seem very confident that even a post-mortem won't reveal any foul play and we don't have any concrete evidence, even though I taped our conversation after you left. There is nothing definite—"

"What about Anna Sophia's testimony?'

'I think she will testify about the medication. She looked as if she had reached her limit when she returned from the hospital, but they might still try to discredit her testimony and blame it all on her.'

'Didn't you overhear her remonstrating with Magdalen when you were hiding in the pharmacy?'

'I did, but I can't prove it was a lethal dose or anything like that, because it wasn't clear enough. And Magdalen knows that. We also have no proof that Magdalen switched the blood tests…'

'OK,' he said, in a thoughtful tone, which she always found reassuring. He was never infected by her panic, always looking for a logical solution.

'I was in touch with the Bishop's Office earlier and briefed them on the relevant sections of the 2020 Regulations. It won't be the Bishop who's coming – probably his Chaplain. What they don't know yet is that we are now looking at a possible murder investigation, not a mere disappearance. Should I tell them? And if so, what can I tell them without prejudicing the investigation?'

'Magdalen could accuse you of bias if you tell them almost anything.'

'That's what I thought, but it's a risky strategy if we let them go in blind. I'm not sure how good the Chaplain is on nuance or complex relationship issues – especially when it comes to dealing with women!'

'But can you trust him to be objective?'

'I think so,' he said carefully, 'but he may be susceptible to someone like Magdalen. Are you happy to tell what you know about the background? It might open things up a bit more, but I don't want to push you further than you are comfortable with.'

'Of course, I will answer anything that helps to reveal the truth about what has happened, but I think the crucial background stuff centres around what happened twenty-odd years ago, after I left, and the dynamic between Maria and Magdalen. We don't really know what led to Maria's breakdown and her year out, but Sarah threw a real hand grenade into the mix on her return from the hospital when she claimed that Maria was almost certainly her birth mother. That was why she was so distraught, as she had been on the brink of telling her when she fell into her coma.'

'You have had a busy night!' he said, quietly. 'How is Sarah?'

'Magdalen has packed her off into a silent retreat, under the pretext of giving her time to grieve, but basically she doesn't want her there when the Bishop or the Chaplain comes.'

'Of course not. She won't want her complicating the issue by opening up a whole new line of enquiry. She will want to be in charge of the agenda. Who was it who made the original complaint?'

'Anastasia.'

'In that case, she will have to be present, but is she up to speed with the latest developments? Otherwise, she will make her case and it will be easily rebuffed.'

'I hadn't thought of that. I will need to get to Anastasia and brief her. What time is it?'

'Ten o'clock. Do you know where her cell is?'

'No, but Anna Sophia will know. I need to get back to the infirmary and ask her. I never thought I would miss mobiles so much!'

'Be careful! Magdalen is likely to be volatile if she feels threatened.'

'No, she and Agnes believe they've got it sewn up. And they may well have... Must go – see you tomorrow. Love you very much.'

She crept down the stairs to the door into the hall and found, to her huge relief, that there was a noticeboard attached to the wall just by the door frame, containing a list of the sisters and guests and the names of their rooms. It was part of a fire notice, which had not even entered her consciousness. Running her finger down the list of names, she found Anastasia's room three doors down from hers on the other side of the corridor and raced up the stairs as quickly as possible, for fear she had already gone to bed.

She knocked as loudly as she dared and Anastasia came sleepily to the door, her auburn hair in a thick plait over her shoulder. Lizzie brought her up to speed rapidly, apologising for coming to her door so late, but reassured by Anastasia's strong response to the shocking news she had to impart.

'Hugh says you will be asked to present the grounds of your complaint to the person they send from the Bishop's Office and it will be up to you initially to make them see that things have changed and you are now deeply concerned about the circumstances of Maria's death. We will support you, but he needs to know this from the complainant. Do you feel OK about doing that? If not, they may win on a technicality. It depends how persuasive Magdalen is and how much they have got to hide.'

'Of course I will do that, but do we have any concrete evidence of foul play?'

'Not enough. Only Anna Sophia's word against theirs. And I am pretty sure that Magdalen will come up with a plausible reason for the change in medication, which appeared to hasten her death. Stepping up the pain relief is the official line from the two of them thus far. Unfortunately, we don't have a post-mortem report yet and, without the Bishop's authority, we have nobody senior enough to instigate anything against the two office holders.'

'So, what are you hoping to get from this meeting?'

'Enough reasonable doubt for the Bishop to authorise a police investigation. Anna Sophia also maintains that they switched the blood samples, so there was no official confirmation that she had leukaemia. Blood transfusions could have saved her and even perhaps given her several years of remission.'

'Right. That is serious stuff. I will certainly do my best to open it up with the Bishop, or whoever comes. I am told it is to be held in the infirmary at 9.30am tomorrow.'

'Yes. See you there.' Lizzie squeezed her arm in thanks and turned back to her room.

CHAPTER SIXTEEN

Next morning, Lizzie got up as soon as her alarm went off and was down in the chapel for 6.30am, feeling an overpowering need to spend the time before Lauds alone with her memories of Maria. 6.30am had been the regular time for her first half hour of silent prayer when she was a novice and it felt like a way of accompanying Maria on her solitary journey, wherever she had got to.

In the night, she had dreamed of her and woken up in tears, with the words from *The Dream of Gerontius* on her lips – *Go forth upon your journey, Christian soul. Go in the name of the Father who created you…* As she sat in her seat in the nave, doing her best to be open before God, she felt flooded with memories of her early days in the novitiate with this kind, good woman, who had tried to put a bridle on her passionate and headstrong charge without breaking her spirit. She remembered her first day in the novitiate, up in the attic of the Sisters' House, when Maria received her into the Community. It was before her 'clothing' as a novice, so she was not presented with the habit and cross and girdle, but she was given a solemn prayer to read out loud like a statement of intent, with Maria as the witness. She could still remember it now: the dark, curtainless attic window, the sensation of her knees on the bare floorboards, the panic at the solemnity and finality of it all, made bearable, almost heroic, by the look on Maria's face:

Take O lord, and receive, my entire liberty
My memory, my understanding, and my whole will.
All that I am, all that I have, thou hast given me,
And I give it back to thee,
To be henceforth disposed of according to thy good pleasure.
Give me only thy love and thy grace,
And I am rich enough,
Nor do I ask anything more

She still had the card, with its beautiful calligraphy, stuck to the inside cover of one of her notebooks from the time, a notebook whose passionate outpourings she was no longer able to read. But Maria's expression endured, as did her faithfulness and humour throughout the two long years of her novitiate. It was only when she took her first vows and moved into Magdalen's sphere of influence that things started to go wrong. Obedience without respect is a twisted thing.

But she still didn't understand what had led to the suicide of her fellow novice, Alexandra. It was clear that she was very homesick and that Magdalen's rejection had devastated her, but it felt like something worse was at the root of it. Was it sexual rather than emotional abuse? Did Maria guess but not act on her suspicions? Why did she blame herself to such an extent that it led to a breakdown?

And what happened in that year away from the Community? Was there a man involved, as Ellen had hinted? Could she conceivably have slept with him? If so, who was he and *where* was he? So many questions and Maria now unable to answer any of them.

For whatever reason, she had come back to the Community. If there was a lover and a baby, they were left behind. What must it have been like to return with those doubly empty hands and then immediately be elected Mother? How did she discipline herself to put one foot in front of the other? Was it an act of expiation? *Take and receive my entire liberty…*

She looked up at the bleached and broken driftwood cross on the choir screen and was more certain than she had ever been about anything that this could not be what was required in the name of love. Her beloved Maria had been crucified for twenty-three years and now she was dead. It wasn't grief, but anger that almost choked her as she waited for the sisters to arrive for Lauds.

But she hadn't expected the full solemnity of Lauds for the Dead, or the reading from Job that broke the early morning silence. The heft of the traditional words from the monastic diurnal fell heavily into the stillness. She looked sideways at Ellen, who was clearly shocked by the radical change of tack, though their office books had been prepared for them by somebody. There was no preamble – just the reading from Job; Anastasia standing in her stall, wearing a black kerchief instead of her usual blue one.

> *My bone cleaveth to my skin and to my flesh, and I am escaped with the skin of my teeth. Have pity on me, have pity on me, O ye my friends; for the hand of God hath touched me. Why do ye persecute me as God, and are not satisfied with my flesh? Oh that my words were now written! oh that they were printed in a book! that they were graven with an iron pen and lead in the rock for ever! For I know that my Redeemer liveth, and that he shall stand at the latter day upon the earth: and though after my skin worms destroy this body, yet in my flesh shall*

I see God: whom I shall see for myself and mine eyes shall behold, and not another; though my reins be consumed within me.

Anastasia read Job's words as if they were a clarion call for justice for her friend and a personal affirmation of her innocence and integrity. Lauds followed in a dignified and respectful fashion, but Lizzie couldn't help but wonder if Magdalen and Agnes had quite registered the impact of allowing Anastasia to read or, for that matter, the impact of the searing words from Lauds of the Dead, which most communities had given up years ago.

She watched Sarah's expression as they worked their way through the psalms and readings, and ached to give her some solace, but there was no respite. The opening antiphon set the scene with *The bones which thou hast broken shall rejoice in the Lord* and hammered home the message with injunctions to *deliver me from blood-guiltiness, O God* and *lo, thou requirest truth in the inward parts.* She could see all the fleeting emotions registering on Sarah's face and was reminded of the play within the play in *Hamlet,* set up specifically to reveal the guilt of the king. Did Magdalen and Agnes not see what they were doing?

The Eucharist was heralded by the muffled bell that they had heard only the day before for Helena. Anastasia officiated, as the resident priest, and Lizzie watched the sisters coming up to the altar rail for Communion, looking more like a defeated army than anything else she could think of. There was an air of pathos and dishevelment about them. They looked motherless, which, of course, they were, despite the presence of both Magdalen and Agnes.

Breakfast was a muted affair, with most of the sisters arriving a lot later than Ellen and Lizzie, and no sign of Sarah. Presumably they had all been to the meeting where they were given the 'facts' about Maria's death. It was hard to sit there and swallow her impulse to stand up and shout out the truth, but she managed it. The crucial thing was to get to that meeting at 9.30am in one piece and ensure that Anastasia was there as the complainant and Anna Sophia as the key witness. She was very aware of the nervousness sitting in the pit of her stomach. So much was unpredictable. So much could go wrong.

She went back to her room to clean her teeth and check her hair and do her best to calm down, before heading out to the infirmary, where she arrived fifteen minutes early. Unfortunately, Hugh had not yet arrived, but he was bringing the Bishop or one of his officers, so would not be early. Happily, Anna Sophia was there and she was able to ask her what she wanted to come out of the meeting. 'A police investigation,' she said immediately. 'A post-mortem that proves Maria was murdered. Somebody needs to stop those two or the Community is lost.'

The next to arrive was Anastasia, who had written down what she wanted to say as the official complainant. Her main job, as she saw it, was to ensure that the Bishop's Office realised they were investigating a potential murder – not a mere disappearance, as she had originally requested. If she could make that clear from the start, she thought they had a chance of the investigation going in the right direction.

But then Magdalen and Agnes arrived, looking not at all flustered, and Lizzie had an awful feeling that they had something up their sleeves. It was such a relief to hear Hugh's familiar voice as he approached through the covered way with a stern-looking grey-haired man in a clerical suit.

CHAPTER SEVENTEEN

It was the hardest thing she had had to do in the Community, sitting through that service, but it felt fitting and strangely confirmed her conviction that she was in the right place. She needed that kind of weight when it came to marking the key moments of transition in life and death. She needed some kind of ritual to say these things matter and anchor them in the ground. There had been nothing like that in her childhood, just fleeting moments of connection, followed by loss and reconnection. Her first foster parents had been lovely, had planned to adopt her, but then her "father" had died suddenly of a heart attack when she was eight. Her mother couldn't cope and had had to give her up. After that, there was a series of different foster families and it didn't work with the kids, probably because she was getting bolshie by then. Eventually, they put her with an older woman called Serena, who was eccentric and single and believed in her for some reason. It was because of her that she joined the church choir and discovered she could sing. The two of them used to go to concerts together and jazz clubs. She even bought her a clarinet.

Serena's church was smoky and dark, full of exotic-smelling incense, candles and icons that pulled at your heart. She became the crucifer and learned how to carry the processional cross at big festivals. The key was behaving as if you were part of the wood. You had to be disciplined – no ego or drama permitted. They used to have visiting preachers from religious communities – often in search of new novices, no doubt, but talking of a depth of commitment and mystical experience that effortlessly filled the hole in her heart.

Maria was one of them, a friend of Serena's from the old days. With hindsight, it was clear to her that Serena brought them together on purpose. She remembered several conversations over a bottle of wine and the look on Serena's face as she listened to them talking animatedly. Did she see the resemblance? Did she know the truth? She was pretty sure that Maria didn't.

Gradually, she had begun to visit Maria at the convent and had experienced the rhythm of the life at first hand. Magdalen, as the novice guardian, had given her some inspirational talks, but it wasn't the talks that did it. It was more an almost tangible sense that the structure of the days slotted into her heart like dovetailing joints and she was where she was meant to be.

Maria had continued to show her what it felt like to be anchored and loved. She couldn't help but wonder if she had promised this to Serena, who died soon after the celebration of her clothing at the convent. Although she had no official role in the novitiate, Maria had always found ways of inventing reasons for them to spend time together, like giving her special lessons on the Rule, or inviting her to lead workshops with novices from neighbouring communities. At the time, Sarah supposed that she could see her isolation as the only novice and didn't want a repeat of what had happened to Alexandra, but perhaps there was more to it.

And now there was hope that the truth would come out. When they were at the hospital, Anna Sophia had heard her tell Maria what she believed to be the truth about their relationship and she had gone to Maria's toilet bag and taken out her hairbrush. Maria had her eyes closed and seemed in a deep coma, but Anna Sophia took her hand and said, 'I am taking a few strands of your hair from this brush, so that I can send them away for a DNA sample. I believe this is what you want…'

It was at that point that the beatific smile spread across Maria's face and she died soon afterwards. It had not seemed necessary to reveal this part of the story to Magdalen and Agnes, but Sarah held it against her heart, knowing that Anna Sophia would find a way to establish the truth.

She might have been banished from the infirmary and sent off into silence, but Anna Sophia had whispered her reassurance that the hair would be sent off for DNA testing that very night. She could only pray that nothing would be allowed to get in the way of that.

Back in her cell, her thoughts strayed constantly to the 9.30am meeting and she found it impossible to stop her fingers from twisting together as she paced backwards and forwards on the bare floorboards.

CHAPTER EIGHTEEN

The stern-looking man in the clerical suit turned out to be the Bishop's Chaplain, who clearly thought he had been sent on a fool's errand and was of a mind to get things over as soon as he decently could. Agnes saw this straightaway and grasped the initiative as soon as they had all taken their seats at the table in the lobby.

'May I introduce myself? I am Sister Agnes, the Assistant Superior of the Community, acting Leader in the absence of Mother Maria—'

'Yes, thank you. I have a few questions I need to ask you,' he replied in an officious tone, ready to embark on his spiel and obviously used to being listened to respectfully.But Agnes was having none of it and interrupted him almost immediately.

'I think you should know before we start,' she declared, briskly, 'that Mother Maria is dead. She died last night. So, I believe your journey has been wasted.'

She moved to get up from her seat, as if to dismiss him, and it was clear that he was rattled and needed time to adjust, which she wasn't going to allow him to have. Magdalen was already holding the door open, but Anastasia had other plans. She put her hand on the Chaplain's arm and said in her best lawyer's voice: 'I am Anastasia, the sister who called your office and made the official complaint about Mother Maria's disappearance, under *The Religious Communities Regulations 2020, The Role of the Visitor, Part 3, Subsection 27.*'

Lizzie inwardly clapped her hands in glee, as she saw his expression grow more solemn.

'I see,' he said, swivelling in his chair to give her his full attention and saying carefully, 'So, I imagine if Mother Maria has died, you have your answer… Am I right?'

'In part, yes, but the circumstances of her death are giving us grave concern and we would like you to authorise a police investigation.'

He barely had time to gulp at this new turn of events before Agnes interjected in her most authoritative tones, 'I'm afraid there is no evidence for such allegations and we already have a post-mortem in train, so there will be no need to take this any further. Thank you so much, Chaplain, and I am sorry we have wasted your time.'

The Chaplain looked from one to the other, apparently relieved that order was restored and began to gather his papers together, when there was another interruption, this time from Anna Sophia. 'I am Sister Anna Sophia and I am the infirmarian here. I was in charge of Mother Maria's care.'

She spoke very quietly and hesitantly, as if the words were being forced out of her with difficulty. Nonetheless, she was about to deliver a vital piece of testimony, despite the forces ranged against her, and Lizzie was full of admiration for her.

They all turned towards her, where she stood with her back to the corridor and her hand on the door jamb, as if she were about to turn tail and flee. Lizzie looked at her set face and suddenly had a bad feeling about what she was going to do. Magdalen had her eyes fixed upon her and Lizzie could see the clenched fist at the end of her right arm, held stiffly at her side. Lizzie tried to make eye contact with her, but she wouldn't raise her eyes.Eventually, she managed to say, 'We gave her diamorphine at the end, to ease her pain, but she was dying anyway. She died of natural causes.'

There was a gasp from everybody in the room except for Agnes and Magdalen, who were smiling with barely suppressed triumph. Anna Sophia had her head down and was backing away down the corridor when Anastasia stood up and said in a voice that brooked no denial, 'Stop, Anna Sophia! I think you have something else to say. Something about Maria's blood tests.'

The Chaplain looked completely nonplussed by this turn of events, unable to decide which direction to look in. Eventually, he said, 'Blood tests?' in a hesitant voice.

They all focused on Anna Sophia. Lizzie prayed that she would have the courage to say what she knew to be the truth, whatever hold Magdalen had over her. Her face reflected the battle going on inside her, but after a painful hiatus, she finally managed to whisper, 'I believe the blood tests were switched, so that we had no official confirmation it was leukaemia and couldn't get her the right treatment.'

'This is a serious charge,' the Chaplain said. 'Who are you accusing?'

'Sister Magdalen,' she mumbled, looking at the floor.

Agnes looked as if a jolt of electricity had gone through her and shot a frantic glance at Magdalen, but she remained completely unruffled and addressed the Chaplain in a calm, matter-of-fact tone, 'I am afraid I was expecting this. Anna Sophia has shown signs of being unstable for a while. I have had to step in on numerous occasions and check that she was administering the right drugs. If you look at the drugs book, you will see my corrections on several pages. I hate to say it, but she has been under a lot of stress lately because of her mother's physical deterioration and it has affected her judgement. She has become forgetful, even paranoid on occasion. Agnes and I were on the point of relieving her of her duties before this happened. I would really like to avoid exposing her to the humiliation of an official investigation, if it could possibly be avoided…' She turned the full force of her charm on the unwitting Chaplain, who instinctively smiled back, reassuringly.

'No!' said Anastasia, looking across at Anna Sophia, who seemed to be shrinking in front of them all. 'Anna Sophia is the best infirmarian we have ever had. I would trust her medical judgement above anyone else's. This is not about her incompetence. This is about a deliberate plot to shorten Maria's life and you mustn't be taken in,' she said forcefully to the Chaplain.

'I'm afraid I can't order an investigation without any evidence to back it up. Do either of you have any concrete evidence to back up your assertions?' he said, taking in both Anna Sophia and Anastasia in a brisk sweep of the room. When nothing was forthcoming, he said, 'Well, I am afraid I will have to wrap up this sorry tale and write my report for the Bishop.' He turned to Magdalen and Agnes, clear relief on his face: 'I suggest that you get a psychological assessment for Sister Anna Sophia and appoint an interim infirmarian. Beyond that, the Community clearly needs to grieve, before such time as you consider filling Maria's place. Thank you. I believe we are done.'

He gathered up his papers and was ushered out by the combined forces of Magdalen and Agnes, who were engaged in animated and smiling conversation with him as they walked through the covered way.

'Smug bastard!' Lizzie spat into the ensuing shocked silence. 'What can we do now?' she asked, despairingly, turning first to Hugh and then to the two sisters.

Anna Sophia surprised her by coming back with a passionate response, 'I hate that woman so much that I don't think I can live this life anymore with a good conscience. But I do have a suggestion.'

They all turned to look at her, amazed at her ability to come up with a plan after Magdalen's demolition job on her.

'The blood test that came back from the lab belonged to a completely healthy woman. If Maria did die of leukaemia, the post-mortem will confirm it and that blood test could not have been hers.'

'OK,' Lizzie said, slowly, as the others nodded in encouragement, 'how can we take this forward? Will the lab still have the blood sample?'

'I am not sure, but we do have their report. If the coroner sees that and compares it with the pathologist's report, then it will be perfectly obvious.'

'But how do we prove who switched them,' Anastasia said, urgently.

'I don't know!' Lizzie said hopelessly.

'Before we do anything, let's look at the report,' Hugh said, quietly. 'I have friends in the pathology department at the hospital. I am sure I can get a professional opinion on the test results without breaking any confidentiality, so that will settle one question, but we still can't prove it was switched.' He turned to Anna Sophia and said, 'When did you send in the blood sample and how was it delivered?'

'Ten days ago. It was couriered in by a local company that Agnes knew.'

'Were you here when it was collected?' he asked.

'Yes, I had it with me in my habit pocket to ensure it wasn't tampered with, as I had my suspicions even then. I handed it over personally to the courier, I'm afraid.' She grimaced.

'Oh!' they all said in unison, letting out a collective sigh.

'Do you know the name of the courier company?' Hugh asked. He seemed calm, but Lizzie could hear the hope draining out of his voice. 'We need to know if they are a legitimate company first and then if there was any opportunity for a switch.'

'I can find out,' she replied, lifting up the pharmacy key from the chain attached to her belt.

They all followed her into the pharmacy, where she quickly located the clean test results, but the daybook containing the courier's name and the time of the collection was missing.

'Did you happen to record in your own notes the time the request was made for the courier?' Hugh asked.

'Yes. It was 3.30pm, ten days ago.'

'We could do a search of all the couriers in the area and their phone records at that time, or we could ask the police to investigate and check out Agnes' phone. Did you see her make the call?'

'Yes, she used a mobile phone.'

'I thought you weren't allowed mobiles?' Lizzie asked in disbelief.

'Oh yes!' Anastasia replied. 'Those at the top have them.'

'Well maybe, just maybe, they will be her nemesis!' Lizzie responded, looking at Hugh for confirmation.

'That's all very well,' he said, 'but we would have to go it alone. The Bishop Visitor won't help us after that little charade. Do we have enough to trigger an investigation?'

As the others looked blank, he continued, 'I think the key piece of evidence is the professional assessment of the discrepancy between the test results. If we can establish that, then we are looking at manslaughter at least, I should think. Possibly murder, if you can have murder by omission…'

'Isn't that what you said, Anna Sophia?' Lizzie asked.

'Yes. It was so clear that she was begging for help, but I just did as I was told. I cannot forgive myself. It was so cowardly.

No better than the camp guards in the concentration camps. Obedience is no defence.'

She spoke with such vehemence and such particularity that Lizzie couldn't help but wonder about her family history and how it was connected with her decision to join the Community. She remembered one old sister from her own time who had entered the Community as an act of expiation for her brother's suicide. It was hard to get inside such an unyielding moral landscape, but it had kept her there for over forty years.

'I will concentrate on getting a professional opinion from my friend in the pathology lab,' Hugh said, as they all shared a much-needed coffee. 'What will you all do? Do you think you'll be put under house arrest?'

His attempt at lightening the mood fell flat and Lizzie stepped in to help, 'I'm going to hide behind Ellen, who will expect her money's worth from the last day of the retreat. Perhaps we can take refuge in the art room again, Anastasia?'

'I'm sure we can find a cupboard for you,' she smiled, 'but what about you, Anna Sophia? They will certainly be coming for you. How can we help?'

'Don't worry about me. I am going to make sure all the records are as secure as I can make them, then I will just sit with my two old sisters in the infirmary and await my fate.'

Her words had the finality of someone with her back against the wall. Lizzie could see her sitting in a chair cradling a shotgun, but decided she had seen too many Westerns and got up to leave with Anastasia and Hugh.

CHAPTER NINETEEN

When she got back to her room in the Sisters' House, she was half expecting a note telling her to vacate it with immediate effect. When there was nothing there, she tried to put herself in Magdalen's and Agnes's shoes. Perhaps the two of them didn't want to arouse suspicion – particularly with Ellen – by doing something that would make them look guilty. They only had to get through this final day of the retreat to emerge with the Community's reputation intact – even if two deaths in four days was a little excessive. She smiled despite the horror and even found some pleasurable anticipation at the thought of how the two of them would spin the recent events to the sisters.

Ellen was waiting for her when she finally got down to her usual seat in the nave. She was puffed up with the importance of her message about the reason for their delayed retreat address. 'The Bishop Visitor has been informed of Mother Maria's death and has sent his Chaplain to arrange the formalities,' she said, officiously. 'Magdalen and Agnes are busy with the arrangements and asked if we would mind another session with Anastasia. I'm happy with that, if you are.'

'Of course,' Lizzie replied, repressing her irritation at Ellen's officiousness. 'Shall we just go to the art room?'

Anastasia was waiting for them, apron on and brushes in her hand, having received her orders from Agnes. How she would have enjoyed being a fly on the wall for that conversation, Lizzie thought to herself, as she sat down at the trestle table where she had previously fashioned her playdough bomb. It already felt like another, more innocent, world.

'I think we need to use this time together to let the shock of Mother Maria's death sink in, don't you?' Anastasia said. 'We can talk first or we can just get on and see what comes out. Is that OK?'

She looked round at her two retreatants, who were both sitting in stunned silence. 'You can use any medium you like – acrylics, pastels, oils, clay. I've laid them all out on the table by the window. Try and get out of your head and into your hands. Say what you need to say through the paint or the clay. It's a much more direct channel.' As she spoke, she was picking up tubes of acrylic paint and a length of cream-coloured cartridge paper, and set about creating a full-length portrait with focus and determination. Was she doing a Banksy for Maria? It might be the only way she had of conveying the truth to the Community if Agnes and Magdalen were keeping a close eye on her. Lizzie went to sit at the other end of Anastasia's table, silently passing her whatever she reached for, impelled to be a witness to whatever she needed to say. She found herself thinking about the role of cartoonists and street artists in Nazi Germany, Northern Ireland or wherever there was oppression and dissent. Was this how Anastasia would use her voice?

Ellen was busy at her table, as usual, and did not seem to be aware of what Anastasia was doing, but Lizzie watched in appalled fascination as a Christa figure emerged, drawn with the sparest of pen lines, echoing the driftwood cross on the choir screen, but also inescapably Maria. The face was gaunt, with deep shadows under the eyes, but it looked out at the viewer with a challenging stare, disturbingly reminiscent of Della Francesca's *Resurrection,* where Christ is climbing out of a stone tomb with judgement on his mind.

Lizzie watched as the turquoise blue of the habit was suggested with a few wispy streaks and the puncture wound in her arm was signalled by a faint trail of blood. It shrieked murder to Lizzie, but perhaps others would see it differently. Then, before her eyes, something else emerged: the outstretched arms took on the welcoming look that was so characteristic of Maria. It was uncanny, as if Anastasia had walked into her heart and painted what was there. She was reduced to shuddering, silent tears. Anastasia squeezed her arm, but said nothing, spraying some fixative on her painting and going across to Ellen's table to do her teacherly thing, without even breaking step.

As they cleared up their things, it was already coffee time, so Ellen disappeared promptly, clutching her painting, and Lizzie was able to follow Anastasia into the kitchen to wash the brushes. 'Where will you hang it?' she said.

'It needs to be somewhere public, so that people have time to react to it before Agnes and Magdalen see it and try to take it down.'

'Do you think the sisters will see it as a call to arms or as an affectionate tribute?'

'I'm not sure. What do you think?' she asked. 'It obviously had an effect on you. Is it too risky?'

Lizzie paused for a moment in her cleaning of the brushes. 'Let me see it again…' She walked back to the table and said, after a minute's reflection, 'I don't know. For me, it is as powerful as Banquo's ghost, but the outstretched arms might be the dominant thing for some people. It depends on who is looking, I suppose.' She photographed it on her phone before adding, 'I have no doubt that Agnes and Magdalen will recognise the message, but maybe that's what you want?'

'Yes, I think it is. It's the only thing I can do for Maria, to honour her memory and try to get justice for her. If it means that I am for the chop, then so be it!' She grinned in a distinctly saturnine way, as she washed the blood-red paint down the sink.

After a quick coffee in the refectory, Lizzie went back to her seat in the nave, with the intention of doing some quiet meditation, but she was distracted by Anastasia hanging up the portrait in a space by the oak door. It was facing the Simpering Statue, and the dialogue between the two of them provoked such dissonance that Anastasia must have thought long and hard about the most provocative place to put it. It was also bang in the middle of the shortcut through the Lady Chapel that most of the sisters took on their way to chapel, so it would not be missed. Midday office was approaching, so Lizzie found herself tense with expectation, waiting for the time bomb to go off.

She was also on edge about the answer to Hugh's enquiry from his pathologist friend. It was the last day of the retreat and if they had no grounds for calling in the police, she would have to pack her bags and leave things in chaos. Not a good thought. Her phone was hidden away in her pocket, but she had her hand on it at all times, waiting for its tell-tale vibration.

The bell went for Sext and None and the sisters started to filter in, some looking startled, struggling to compose their faces, and some looking as absent and spaced-out as they had at Lauds. The shock was seeing Sarah, who was sitting in her stall, openly weeping and looking round distractedly as if searching for someone, anyone, who could explain what was happening. Nobody was paying her any attention and Lizzie could hardly restrain herself from rushing in and pulling her out. Why did she choose to sit there, despite everything?

Both Magdalen and Agnes were there, in the Superiors' stalls, on either side of the empty Mother's seat. They were both past masters of presenting serene exteriors and today was no different, though Lizzie could see a pulse throbbing in Magdalen's cheek, as if she was grinding her teeth.

Save me, Oh Lord, from the lion's mouth
Thou hast heard me also from among the horns of the unicorns

The plainchant washed backwards and forwards across the space between the two Superiors and their sisters, huddled in their unforgiving stalls.

Yea the waters had drowned us * and the stream had gone
 over our soul
The deep waters of the proud * had gone even over our soul

It was very noticeable to Lizzie that the chant had lost its rhythm and they were stumbling over the pause in the middle of each verse of the psalms, unable to synchronise their responses – such a sure indication of unease in a praying community.

Was she imagining it, or were they all waiting for a sign that someone was going to lead them out of this morass? She found herself instinctively looking to Anastasia, but she was a marked woman now. How long would it be before she was disappeared or dead?

She needed to check on both Anna Sophia and Sarah, but Sarah had to be the priority in case she was spirited away again. Lizzie knew she had two minutes at most when they filed out of chapel, as the Superiors went one way and the sisters another. She waited by the Simpering Statue and whispered to Sarah who was at the back of the line, 'Hugh is checking the blood sample sent to the lab. If his pathologist friend says it comes from a healthy person, it proves that the samples were switched and we can call in the police.'

Sarah began to reply, but saw Magdalen rounding the corner and made to flee. 'Leave me a message at lunch,' Lizzie whispered, immediately veering off in the other direction, and doing a wide circuit before returning to the lunch queue outside the refectory.

It was her favourite lunch – homemade bread, cheese, dates and apples. She had just picked up her coffee from the urn and returned to her solitary table when she saw a small piece of paper poking out from her side plate. 'Meet me in the hermitage straight after this,' it said in scrawled handwriting.

It felt dangerous and she was scared for Sarah, but she went all the same, taking care to cover her tracks.

She was waiting behind the door. 'Who did the painting? It was so powerful! Was it Anastasia?'

'Yes. It was ridiculously brave, but I think she felt she had to do something to challenge Magdalen's version of events.'

'It certainly does that, but they won't let it go. I am going to take it down off the wall as soon as I get back and hide it somewhere.'

'Be careful!'

She looked older somehow and more resolved. She was wearing a white kerchief, though it was not a part of the uniform, as if she wanted to say that she was taking her commitment more seriously from now on. Lizzie was surprised, expecting her to be more alienated, rather than less, after the way she had been treated.

She saw Lizzie's eyes going to the kerchief and said, 'It's not because of Magdalen. It's despite her. I want to live the life with integrity, whatever it costs.' Her eyes held a crusader glint, making Lizzie feel her age and suddenly nostalgic for her settled life with Hugh.

'I am waiting to hear from Hugh about the blood sample. If we get the go-ahead, Anastasia will call in the police.'

'You might have to protect her till then. And Anna Sophia, too,' Sarah said with a shudder. 'She took a sample of hair from Maria's brush when we were in the hospital and she whispered to me later that she had sent it away for DNA testing, so we are waiting for *two* important test results.' She smiled, despite herself.

'You'd better go now,' Lizzie said. 'You are supposed to be in silent retreat. Will you be alright?'

'Yes. I'll be OK. When do you think Hugh will get word from his pathologist friend?'

'He thought within a few hours, as he only needs to confirm that they are healthy test results. Go now!' Lizzie said, giving her a little push. 'We don't want to give them any grounds for worse sanctions against you.'

After a brief hug, Sarah melted away into the shrubbery and Lizzie made her way cautiously round the back of the building towards the infirmary, her senses alert for any indication that she was being followed.

CHAPTER TWENTY

Anna Sophia must have been watching out for her, as she came to the door very rapidly, immediately pressing for any news on the test results.

'Not yet. How are you? Have Magdalen and Agnes been over?' she asked, anxiously.

'No, it's been quiet. Sit with me, will you? Have a coffee. I want to tell you something.'

They sat in a corner of the lobby where they were hidden from the garden and Anna Sophia began to talk:

'I don't think I have long—'

'We won't let them hurt you!' Lizzie interrupted.

'No, I don't mean that. I just have a feeling that my time has come. I need to explain, so that someone at least knows my story...'

There was a dignity and finality in the way she spoke that silenced Lizzie's attempt at reassurance and she simply waited for what was coming next.

'My mother was a Polish Jew, sent to Auschwitz-Birkenau in 1944 at the age of seventeen. She managed to get herself made a *Kapo,* or overseer, of other female prisoners, responsible for their work quotas. It involved a lot of beatings (often to death) of starving and exhausted women, but she hardened herself against it because it was a way of surviving, giving her better food and special privileges. She never showed any remorse – triumph, if anything, at her own ingenuity in managing to survive.

The guilt in me grew as I became a teenager and gradually pieced together her history. She had no family in England and it soon became clear that she had arrived in the country as a refugee and changed her name to escape detection. She never admitted it in so many words, but I suspect she had a lover who was one of the SS officers in the camp. That may have been the real reason she survived – unthinkable as it is. She was a beautiful woman, my mother, despite all. Anyway, she somehow managed to get a job as a librarian at a minor public school, where she could live in. The headmaster was sympathetic to exiles, as he was one himself, and the school paid for her training. She very quickly married my father, the school classics master, and set about the business of merging into English society. When I was born, in 1954, she was already an integral part of the school fabric and I was eligible for free schooling, the prep and then the senior school. She wasn't a natural mother, but my father was a lovely man – gentle and thoughtful. I grew up a good Anglican, with a very tender conscience, and went off to train as a nurse at the Middlesex in London. The first time I encountered a nun – she was a Chaplain at the hospital – I was hooked. It was the guilt, you see. A perfect fit.'

'Did your mother ever speak about the conditions in the camps?'

'No, but she was always strange about food. Ate ridiculously fast and would never share anything. Had a thing about fresh bread. It was only when she got dementia and started to talk obsessively about mouldy bread that I researched the conditions in the camps and learned the truth about their starvation rations.'

'I remember when I first came,' Lizzie said, 'the really keen novices used to eat mouldy bread to show how ascetic they could be…'

'Yes,' she said. 'It was the ones who had never been hungry.'

There was a long pause, as if Anna Sophia was psyching herself up for something. 'I am wondering,' Lizzie said, after a bit, 'if all this has something to do with Magdalen and the hold she has over you. Is this the shame your mother couldn't survive?'

'Yes, though it won't be long before she forgets who she is, so it will cease to matter.'

'I see.'

'But it's more than that. I have spent thirty years in this community. I have kept the infirmary running sweetly for all those years and now Magdalen accuses me of negligence. I cannot bear it. And I cannot bear that Magdalen is likely to become the next Mother. It is a travesty of everything the Community stands for. They have been my family. Maria has been my moral compass. It is not right that the person who murdered her should be allowed to take her place.'

As she spoke, her accent seemed to change and something of her Polish origins could be heard in her voice. It wasn't just her accent, but a kind of passionate intensity that was foreign to the average English person. Lizzie was unsure how to react, beyond nodding in agreement, so asked, 'How did Magdalen learn about your mother's background?'

'When she was a novice, she spent a couple of weeks in the infirmary with glandular fever. I was just beginning to uncover the enormity of my mother's background and shared a lot of it with her. She was so kind and supportive. I don't know how I would have got through it without her, but then she changed.'

'What changed?'

'It started with Alexandra's suicide. I think she knew her own part in it, because she had talked of how she couldn't bear it when people got clingy, but she saw how easy it was to twist the blame onto Maria and accuse her of not taking enough care of a vulnerable novice. Maria always had a very soft heart and took the blame on herself to the extent that she had a breakdown, as you know.'

'But you said something about a man—'

'Yes, it was the Chaplain General of the Community, a high-ranking priest from a neighbouring monastery, who was involved in the novice's funeral and was available for the sisters to talk to. Both Maria and Magdalen saw him, and it was clear that Magdalen was affronted by his preference for Maria. She wasn't used to it, you see. She was used to dazzling all comers.

Nothing was ever said, but I am clear that he took advantage of Maria's inexperience and grief and got her to sleep with him – maybe just for comfort, who knows – but she had broken her vow of chastity, so she must have been racked with guilt. He left his community soon after and disappeared, leaving her to bear the brunt. She took time out for a year, ostensibly to recover from the breakdown that ensued, but it seems highly probable now that she had a baby, which she gave away for adoption.'

'And that was Sarah?'

'Possibly, yes. I have sent the hair from Maria's brush away for DNA testing and asked them to send the result to your email address, for safety's sake. I hope that's OK.'

'Of course. But I still don't understand Magdalen's role in all this.'

'I don't get how she managed it, but Magdalen found out about the pregnancy somehow and threatened to expose her.'

'But why did she want to come back? Why didn't she keep the baby and apply to be dispensed from her vows?'

'Shame. I think it was shame. The father didn't want to know. Her own mother disowned her. She had broken her vows. I think it was all too much, on top of her guilt about Alexandra's death.'

'So, she sacrificed herself, and the baby, to work off her shame?'

'That's about right. And Magdalen held it over her and used it to get herself in a position of power.'

'But then it all went pear-shaped, because the Community voted for her to be the next Mother when Mother Cicely died!'

'Yes, so she became Magdalen's puppet, until she decided she had waited long enough and Maria would have to be got rid of.'

'It all sounds very gothic! Do you really believe that someone so beautiful in body and soul could turn into such a monster?'

'Well, my mother did…'

They both sat in silence for a few minutes, then Lizzie said, 'So you reckon that Magdalen was willing to murder Maria to get the position of power she craved?'

'Yes, I do, and I have seen it with my own eyes, though technically it's murder by omission, as Hugh himself acknowledged.'

'So, what will you do if we can't find the evidence to prove it?'

'I have nothing to lose. That makes me dangerous. My mother's dementia is now so far advanced that she soon won't care about anything, so I will do whatever it takes to see that justice is done.'

The image of her sitting, waiting, with the gun in her lap, flashed into Lizzie's mind again, and she remembered Anna Sophia's facility with the hypodermic. For the first time, she felt it was all too big for her to handle and she had poked her stick into something much more primitive and powerful than she had ever anticipated. 'We need that result from the pathology lab, then we can call the police in,' she said, briskly, trying to bring things down to an everyday level.

'Yes,' Anna Sophia replied. 'See if you can hurry things up.' She smiled wearily, as if she didn't hold out much hope.

Lizzie went out into the garden, looking for a spot with good mobile coverage, so that she could call Hugh again. Down by the boundary wall, she got two bars and called him. 'I was just trying to call you,' he said. 'My friend, John, came up with the confirmation we needed. It was a healthy blood sample, so we need to contact the police. Someone from the Community needs to do it. Anastasia?'

'Yes. I think she is the best person. Have you got anywhere with courier firms and the 3.30pm booking?'

'No, I have done a comprehensive sweep of all the firms in the area and nothing. I think Agnes must have organised it through personal contacts.'

'So, we have to get the police to examine her phone records. What if she has wind of what we're doing and erases the texts?'

'I think they can still recover them.'

'It's a big deal to call in the police.'

'I know. You need to talk to Anastasia and see if she is willing to go through with it.'

'I think if she doesn't, Anna Sophia might administer her own rough justice. I've just been speaking with her and I think she may be at the end of her rope.'

'Oh! Speak to Anastasia as soon as you can then!'

'Today is the last day of the retreat, Hugh. I will have to leave after breakfast tomorrow, so I'm scared about the outcome.'

'Not sure that the police can be made to move that quickly. Is there anyone nearby you could stay with?'

'Not that I can think of. There's a B&B opposite, if it comes to it. I'll go and find Anastasia now. Speak soon. Love you.'

It was reassuring to hear his voice, as she was left with a heavy feeling after Anna Sophia's revelations. She made her way through the door into the sacristy and then through into the main house where the art room faced her. Anastasia opened the door instantly at her knock and drew her inside, her face full of questions.

'We need to contact the police straightaway,' Lizzie said without preamble. 'The blood sample is a healthy one. Are you still up for it? I know it's a massive step.'

Anastasia closed a few remaining cupboard doors and began washing her hands as she considered her response. 'Maria would never forgive us if we let her down now. We owe it to her.'

'I agree, but I've got a home to go to. It feels like we are about to bring the roof down over all your heads and I'm really scared for you.'

'Don't be. It's long overdue and we will survive it and rebuild. There are some good people in this community.'

'I think Sarah will be one of them,' she said in answer. Anastasia nodded her head and smiled, 'I think so, too. There's a phone in the community room. Follow me.'

CHAPTER TWENTY-ONE

He was only too aware that time was running out for them to find the evidence of the switch, and, even then, there was no certainty that the police would act. Once they could legitimately oust Lizzie from the premises, he had a horrible feeling that the Community would just close its doors and smother the truth by depriving it of oxygen. Lizzie had often told him about the almost Byzantine lengths they would go to when they wanted to deny the existence of an uncomfortable truth. He had never really understood the power of obedience, as logic and enquiry were second nature to him, but Lizzie had always defended its ability to strip the ego of its pretensions. She had often talked about the *cleanness* of "having nothing yet possessing all things" – a mantra repeated in the Novitiate – and maintained that the vows could bring about this state, like bones picked clean.

All very well for the vow of poverty and possessions, but not obedience and the will, as far as he was concerned. He had encountered quite a few of the old-style Reverend Mothers in his role at Church House and he would not have enjoyed falling into their clutches. For every wise old bird, there were at least three ferocious matriarchs.

But it was always possible that he was wrong – he knew that – and Lizzie was able to make herself open and vulnerable in a way that he couldn't. All his years at boarding school had taught him nothing if not survival and you didn't survive by making yourself vulnerable. But he also knew that his survival strategies made it hard for her to get close to him and she suffered from that.

She was very vulnerable now and he knew only too well that she needed this convent thing to come to a good end. If justice was not done, she would be left bleeding, with little hope of the old wounds healing. It was up to him to fix it. But how? He must know someone in the police who would give them a sympathetic hearing…

CHAPTER TWENTY-TWO

The community room was thankfully unlocked and the phone was sitting on the table by the window. Anastasia strode straight to it and picked up the receiver in a determined way, but there was no dialling tone. Of course! Rule number one: cut off the phone connections. Agnes and Magdalen were probably smiling gleefully at the thought that they had pre-empted their next move. The idea that mobile phones were ubiquitous in the outside world had probably never occurred to them.

Lizzie opened up her mobile and was about to dial 999 when an urgent message came through from Hugh: 'This is the man to call. He owes me a favour. Mention my name. He is minutes away at the city police station.'

She wrote down the name and number and passed the phone to Anastasia, reading out the digits as she tapped them in. 'What is your surname – Hugh's name – when they ask me?' Anastasia said, hurriedly. Surnames were an irrelevance in Community, so she would never have known even her maiden name. You were given your new name in Community and your old identity fell away, along with your birthday and most of your history. She had always found it hard that birthdays weren't celebrated. Celebrating your saint's day really didn't cut it in her book.

The phone was ringing out, but no answer. What if he was on holiday or out of the office on a case? How long should they wait?

Eventually, a gruff voice answered, 'Hello. Peter Browning speaking.' Anastasia put him on speakerphone, as demonstrated by Lizzie, so she could hear the brisk impatience in his voice. She hoped he wasn't fiercely anti-religious or they had no chance.

Anastasia did not seem intimidated by his voice and was herself quite brisk and to the point. 'Hugh Ferguson advised us to contact you, as we have evidence of an attempted murder within the Community and we need your help.'

There was a pause while he was clearly weighing up how seriously he should take her accusation. 'Can you give me your name and a bit more detail, please, then I can see how we could help.'

'Of course. I am Sister Anastasia, one of the senior sisters here. Our Mother Superior has just died and we have reason to believe that the Assistant Superior and the Novice Guardian are behind her death.'

'I see,' he said, after a pause. 'What grounds have you got for this belief?'

'She died of acute leukaemia and our infirmarian claims that the blood sample she sent to the lab to test for leukaemia was switched, so that the test came back negative and she did not get the treatment that might have saved her.'

'There are two points here,' he said, cautiously. 'One is your word "might", which seems to imply that she could have died even with the right treatment. The other is your evidence for claiming the sample was switched. Can you help me with either of those?' He had on his patient voice, which Lizzie hoped was genuine.

Anastasia was unfazed and carried on, like the great lawyer she might have been. 'Your friend, Hugh, has consulted a contact in the local pathology lab and shown him the test results, asking him to state whether they could have been the results of someone with advanced leukaemia. Apparently, that is an impossibility. They are the results of a completely healthy individual. As to your question whether she could have died anyway, the answer is certainly she could, but with the right treatment – such as blood transfusions – she might have had several years of remission.'

'Can you prove they were switched and who by?'

'We know they were not tampered with before they were picked up by the courier at 3.30pm on November 30th and we know that Sister Agnes booked the courier on her mobile, but we don't have the name of the courier, and the daybook that would normally record this is missing.'

'So, you want us to go through Sister Agnes's phone records? It would have to be part of an official investigation. Data protection prevents us from doing it without official sanction. Are you willing to have an investigation disrupting the Community? It will be very intrusive.'

'Yes! Mother Maria needs justice.'

'OK. Leave it with me. I will see what I can do.'

There was a loud click at the other end as he put the phone down and the look the two women exchanged was not hopeful. 'I'm not convinced he wants to take it on, are you?' Lizzie said.

'No. Hard to pin down why. Something in his tone. I suspect he thinks we're being hysterical. Hothouse emotions and all that. It's quite a common reaction.'

'I know. So, what next? Do we see if Hugh has any ideas or do we try and fix it ourselves?'

'It would be good to see it through to the end ourselves.

But before we burn our boats, shall we give the Detective Inspector a head start and see what he can come up with?'

'I agree. It's 2.30pm now. Let's give him till 4pm. In the meantime, I think we need to make a more thorough search for that daybook and also see if Anna Sophia can give us a description of the courier she gave the sample to.'

'OK, meet you there as soon as I have cleared up here.'

'You know,' Anastasia said, quietly, her eyes focused on her paints and brushes as she started to tidy up, 'we don't yet know who provided the healthy sample…'

Lizzie paused, with her hand on the door handle. 'I know. I have always assumed it was Magdalen, but we don't actually know, do we? Presumably, you need a certain amount of skill to take a blood sample?'

'That's what I was thinking,' Anastasia said, without looking up.

Lizzie made her way quickly into the garden and headed for the covered way, her mind full of jumbled pieces, which refused to come together to form a coherent picture. At the same time, she was aware of an errant piece that she was not willing to allow into the frame.

As she got nearer, she could see Anna Sophia pacing up and down in the lobby and then rushing to the door when she spotted Lizzie's arrival.

'No news yet,' she said. 'We are waiting for the police to decide how to take things forward. We need that daybook. I have come to help you have another look.'

For the next five minutes, Lizzie scoured the office and the pharmacy, opening every cupboard, drawer and cabinet, Anna Sophia following listlessly behind her. Finally, Lizzie stood still and turned to face her new friend. 'There never was any daybook, was there?'

'No,' Anna Sophia replied. After a lengthy pause, she

continued: 'There's only me here, so no need for it. I have a drugs book and the rest is in my diary.'

'So why did you say that there was?'

'I don't know. I think I thought it would look more efficient if there was one and the pick-up time was recorded in it.'

'So, when did you take the blood sample from Maria?'

'About 2.30pm that day. It's recorded in the drugs book.'

'And you kept the sample in the pocket of your habit, so it wasn't tampered with?'

'Yes,' she said, uneasily, 'after I'd made her comfortable. I've told you all this before. Where are you going with this?'

'It's just that I've found myself wondering who took the other blood sample – the one that was switched. It seems to me quite a skilled operation…'

'I don't know,' she said, defensively.

'Hugh has researched all the courier companies in the area and there are no pick-ups booked for 3.30pm. The next step is to seize Agnes's phone and check her calls. Do you think they will find anything?'

'No,' she said, lifting her head to look Lizzie straight in the face. 'They didn't want to leave any traces. I was made to make the call.'

'On which phone?'

'The landline here.'

'OK. That's a lot of misinformation. An outsider might think you were colluding with this whole sorry deception. Why, Anna?'

'Very simple. She would expose my mother. I couldn't let that happen, could I, Judas that I am?'

Shame was the word hanging in the air between them and Lizzie had a horrible sense that there was worse to come.

Anastasia chose that moment to come rushing in. Her eyes took in the gravity of the scene and her first words were,

'Was it you then, Anna? Was it your blood? You need to be straight with us, as it will all come out, once the police start their investigation.'

Anna Sophia's face crumpled, but there were no tears. It was almost as if it was a relief. The words tumbled out as if a stone had been removed. 'Blood will have blood, won't it? It was my blood that killed her. I don't deserve to live.' She stared straight ahead, refusing to meet their eyes.

Anastasia moved to her side and put her hand on her arm, as if to steady her. 'Just tell us what happened, Anna.'

'Magdalen said that the Community couldn't survive a long period of instability, that we needed a strong leader to make the changes that were needed. She said that Maria was going to die anyway, so we were just shortening her suffering. She was very persuasive. I almost believed her.'

'Yes, I know what that's like,' Lizzie muttered under her breath.

Anna Sophia looked at her hopefully, as if she had found somebody who understood, but instead Lizzie said, 'So *you* did the switch? Where did you put the real sample?'

'In the safe. I couldn't bring myself to throw it away.'

'So, all the evidence is there. Which courier did you use?'

'I took it myself. Magdalen paid for a taxi. She wanted to be sure it got there safely and I knew my way around.'

'But how could you?' Lizzie said, aware that her voice was full of incredulity – and anger.

'I told myself it wouldn't make any difference, that she would die anyway, and I could make up for it by looking after her when she was dying…'

'And if you had refused to do it?'

'Magdalen said she would expose my mother in the local newspaper. She even showed me the piece she had written. It would have killed her.'

Lizzie and Anastasia looked at each other, both unsure what to do next. Anna Sophia looked from one to the other, then stepped forward with her wrists outstretched: 'I am ready. Call the police!'

It was an answer of sorts, but it wasn't justice. Both of them hung back.

'We need to speak to Hugh,' Lizzie said, after a moment. 'We need a calmer perspective. Shall I call him?' she asked Anastasia.

'Yes!' she responded immediately. 'Have you got any brandy, Anna, in that filing cabinet of yours? I think we need something.'

The pair of them went off in search of glasses while Lizzie texted her SOS to Hugh. It was 4pm, but tea was not on the horizon.

CHAPTER TWENTY-THREE

In less than twenty minutes, Lizzie heard Hugh's car and went out to meet him at the gate, so that she could bring him up to date before he encountered Anna Sophia. They kept to the path through the shrubbery to avoid being spotted, though Lizzie knew they would be exposed when they crossed the lawn leading to the covered way.

His reaction showed how blindsided he was by the latest developments. 'I really don't know where that leaves us, do you, Liz? A very clever ploy by Magdalen. Puts her at an even further remove from the actual deed. It was going to be hard enough to get her on manslaughter. Does *conspiracy to murder* work for manslaughter? I don't know.' He ran his fingers restlessly through his short, dark hair, which, as usual, was sticking up in all directions. 'Perhaps *blackmail* or *coercion*. I don't know. I'm out of my depth, I'm afraid. Did you speak to Peter?'

'I did, but I'm not sure he's onside. You may get a call from him, though I strongly suspect it will go in the OBI drawer.'

'OBI?'

'Oh, bugger it!' She grinned.

'Oh yeah! The one your father had at work.'

'Exactly.'

They had reached the entrance to the covered way and slipped in as rapidly as they could. Anastasia and Anna Sophia were sitting in the leather bucket chairs in the lobby, companionably sipping their brandy like the two old friends they were. Anastasia's hair had been released in its customary plait down her back and Anna Sophia was curled up, with her legs tucked under her. Lizzie and Hugh sat down and listened in on a conversation that appeared well established. 'So, as I see it, Anna, we are in a bit of a dilemma. It is clear now that the blood sample was switched, which led to at least a hastening of Maria's death, so there is a criminal case to answer. You can go ahead and confess to your part in it, but there is a risk that Magdalen will get away with it because she has covered up her tracks so well. This means that justice will not have been served and you will have been made the scapegoat – possibly going to prison. That doesn't sit well with me.

Alternatively, we can administer our own form of justice here in Community. We can give her the option of acknowledging her guilt and standing down from all forms of office in the Community or the alternative of brazening it out with the police and risking that our evidence will convict her. Either way, she will face some form of justice. What do you think?'

'If I thought she might show any kind of acknowledgement or repentance, I might be tempted to go the Community route, but it would need to be public. The Community would have to hear the unvarnished truth.'

'Yes, I agree. Nothing less.'

'But is she capable of that kind of self-knowledge, humility even?'

'She was once,' Lizzie said, from deep in her own bucket chair. 'There was a grace and a brightness about her that was almost angelic. Then things started to go bad on her. I have an awful feeling we have to give her a chance to redeem herself, don't we?'

'Perhaps. But what if she lies to us and doesn't mean it at all?' Anna Sophia said. 'It's cleaner to let the police deal with it. I'm ready.' She held out her wrists again, almost as if she was hungry for handcuffs to bite into her flesh.

'And what about forgiveness, old friend?' Anastasia said, patting her arm. 'No malice aforethought. Just fear and coercion. Can you not live with that? I think Maria would have forgiven you had she known what was going on.' They all nodded their agreement, even Lizzie, won over by the compassion in Anastasia's voice.

'Watch out!' Hugh suddenly said in a loud stage whisper, jumping up from his chair. 'Bandits at 12 o'clock!'

They all turned to the window and recoiled from the sight of Magdalen bearing down on them like an avenging angel. *She must have been watching from the sacristy*, Lizzie thought.

Hugh was already on his feet and met her at the door, working hard to diffuse her hostility, but she batted him out of the way and made straight for Anna Sophia.

'I was hoping to see you alone, but this cannot wait, so I am afraid the others will have to hear it.' She came over to Anna Sophia's chair, looming over her as she spoke. 'I have just heard from the local police, who are initiating an investigation into Mother Maria's tragic death. I imagine you are behind this?' she said, accusingly, not waiting for the answer. 'Regrettably, that means I will have to tell the truth about your part in this sad tale. Do your friends know, for instance, that it was you who switched the blood samples?' she asked, like someone laying down the winning hand in poker.

'Yes, actually we do!' Anastasia replied, calmly. 'And we also know that it was her blood in the sample that was sent.'

Lizzie watched in fascination as Magdalen adroitly

switched tack and continued, 'I see that she has told you some of the story, but not all. Did she tell you that she did it to cover up her own criminal negligence, that she had misdiagnosed Maria from the start and didn't want her incompetence to be revealed?'

'No! That is not true, Magdalen! You know that I did it because you were blackmailing me.'

'I am afraid there is no evidence for that, is there, Sister? I was going along with it solely to protect your reputation and I shall tell the police that.

I shall also tell them that you have been displaying symptoms of paranoia for the last few months – just like your mother. The nurses from her care home will corroborate that, so I am afraid your argument will not stand up to scrutiny in a court of law.' She turned to look at them all, opening her arms wide, as if to say "QED".

It was clear from her body language and her tone of voice that she had convinced herself of the truth of this twisted version of events, which scared Lizzie more than anything else, because if *she* was convinced then any jury would be. Such was the power of her charm.

At this point, Anastasia stood up and began walking around, as if she were counsel for the defence, preparing her cross-examination of a hostile witness. She came and stood opposite Magdalen, squaring her shoulders as she did so, then surprised them all with the following proposal. 'You might be right, Magdalen, that your version of the truth is enough to convince a jury, but we want to appeal to you at a deeper level and give you the opportunity to recover the self who came into this community with a genuine vocation for the religious life.

You might win in a court of law and succeed in putting your sister in prison, but we would like to offer you a different kind of success, that of working out your redemption in penitence and humility. If you acknowledge what you have done, confess it publicly to your sisters and step down from all higher office, then we promise not to pursue the police investigation, which we have reason to believe we would win.'

They all turned to Magdalen in appalled fascination, as if the fate of the world were in her hands. Would she press the nuclear button or would she pull back from the brink? Lizzie watched the expressions flitting across her face, like sunlight and clouds chasing each other, and realised she was holding her breath with the uncertainty of the outcome.

Finally, after what seemed like hours, but was probably only seconds, she spoke, standing behind one of the empty chairs, with her hands resting on the back. The battle was over.

'I am afraid I am honour-bound to pursue the truth in this matter and that means exposing Anna Sophia's negligence. Otherwise, she will be a risk to the whole community, which could result in another death. I will be gathering my evidence to present to the police and now I must leave you to attend to that promptly. Goodbye, Lizzie. You will be leaving tomorrow.'

She began to move towards the door, but Anna Sophia blocked her way. And there it was, the revolver in her hand. Lizzie had no doubt that it would have come from her mother. It would be the weapon of choice and she would have kept it well-oiled and in working order.

'I'm afraid I can't let you get away with it, Magdalen. When it comes to the crunch, I seem to have found my courage. So here we are! I owe it to my mother and to myself to defend the truth and I owe it to Maria to give her justice, if the system cannot.'

She raised the gun and Hugh launched himself at her, but it was too late. She saw him out of the corner of her eye and side-stepped before steadying her arm and shooting Magdalen twice through the heart. While they were all still in shock, she turned the gun on herself and shot herself through the roof of her mouth. There was no mistake. They were both killed instantly.

The scene was like the end of a Greek tragedy with the corpses piled up and blood spattered everywhere. Shocking and surreal though it was, there was also a terrible inevitability about it. Magdalen had pushed and pushed and not seen the signs in Anna Sophia's face. Those ancient Greek writers had words for things like that.

Lizzie went and looked down at the two of them, so newly dead, in appalled fascination. She had no tears. Perhaps shock did that to you. She hoped so. The others looked similarly paralysed – as if the music had stopped and they had all been left like statues.

Even in death, Magdalen's face was beautiful, her expression mildly surprised, whereas one half of Anna Sophia's face was blown away, with shattered bone exposed. Their habits looked so incongruous, with bloodstains spreading over them, that you couldn't help but think that the actors would get up any minute to take their bow.

Anastasia was the first to recover and moved to cover their faces in a show of respect, but Hugh put out his hand to stop her. 'This is a crime scene now. We mustn't touch anything. I will call the police.'

CHAPTER TWENTY-FOUR

Once Hugh had completed his call, they all moved back to the kitchen area and laid out three stacking chairs to sit on while they waited. Three didn't seem enough. Lizzie found herself checking and rechecking that they hadn't missed anyone out as she put the kettle on and set out the mugs. Anastasia disappeared for a minute, to check on the two infirm sisters at the end of the corridor, fearing they might have been disturbed. Luckily, they were both asleep, so she was quick to return.

It felt deeply bizarre to be sitting there, drinking tea, while two of their friends were lying dead at their feet. Lizzie was very conscious that she and Hugh now outnumbered the Community members and was troubled by the thought that she might have been the catalyst for three deaths. She instinctively pulled her chair closer to Hugh's and sought his hand silently.

Anastasia was clearly worrying about how the Community would react and what she should say. Hugh was thinking about the power vacuum now Magdalen was gone and where Agnes would position herself if she was Magdalen's co-conspirator. Anastasia would need some support to face her down. Should he and Lizzie stay on for a bit? Would they be welcome?

All of their thoughts were savagely interrupted by a commotion at the door, as five police marched in, with Pete Browning at their head. He nodded at Hugh, before introducing himself and his team. He looked very sheepish, as if he realised that his lack of interest earlier had been noted, but the team got to work straightaway, the two forensics taking photographs and measuring blood spatters, bagging the gun and bringing it over to their boss to examine more closely. Guns were clearly a speciality of his and he quickly identified it as a Luger P08, manufactured by Mauser and used by the Waffen-SS. Hugh looked at him with interest, then quickly turned to Lizzie to ask her if she had any ideas of its origin.

'A trophy of Anna-Sophia's mother, I would guess. She was in Auschwitz-Birkenau and Anna Sophia was pretty sure she slept with an SS officer as a means of survival. It doesn't surprise me at all that she would use it for her instrument of revenge. It must have seemed perfect…'

Anastasia nodded in agreement and Detective Inspector Browning had the grace to look shocked. *His cynicism was not total then*, Lizzie thought to herself, as a wave of exhaustion and grief hit her and she prayed that the police interviews would not be dragged out. At least there was no doubt about the perpetrator, though her motives might take a little longer to unravel.

Anastasia asked if she might be interviewed first, as she would need to speak to the Community, but it was agreed that the DI and his two female officers would save time by taking all their statements simultaneously in separate rooms. Despite Anastasia's request that they be allowed to prepare the bodies for burial, the DI was adamant that they would have to be taken to the pathology lab for a post-mortem, as required for any violent death. He did, however, concede that it would probably be a quick turnaround, as the cause of death was undisputed and confirmed by three separate witnesses.

Lizzie found herself wondering how they would do the overnight vigil in chapel. Would the murderer and victim lie side by side? And in the final analysis, who was the murderer and who the victim? It was hard to look at their faces – particularly Anna Sophia's – but before they were taken away by the forensic team, she managed a brief caress of Magdalen's cheek in a gesture of farewell. It was jarringly cold, but somehow more accessible in death than it ever was in life. She was aware of Hugh's gaze on her and knew that he would be there for her, as he always had been, even if he did not fully understand. She was almost felled by her longing to go home with him and let it all fall away, but there was more to do and she knew they needed to be there to support Anastasia – and Sarah, too. And there was also the question of Agnes. The body bags were zipped up and removed and the police gone with them, promising to return in the morning. Vespers was almost upon them and Anastasia was clearly girding herself up for an unimaginable announcement. How on earth did you tell your sisters that two of them had suffered a violent death and one at the hands of the other?

'I am just trying to think what kind of service could possibly meet the need,' Anastasia said, turning to Lizzie, a heavy sigh weighting her voice. 'I thought possibly the *Lamentations* we do on Maundy Thursday. Do you remember? We used to call it *Tenebrae* – the one where the candles are gradually put out, one after every psalm. It has the emotional heft we need somehow, but I'm not sure. What do you think?'

'I remember the deep impression it had on me – not just the penitential psalms and the words of Jeremiah, but the deepening darkness as the candles went out one by one. But...'

'I know. The penitential psalms can carry the weight, but

everybody will be feeling so shocked and overwhelmed. Maybe even guilty. We need something more personal, something that allows them to express the complexity of their feelings.'

'Yes and we don't have long before the sisters will be gathering for Vespers. I think we need something simpler and more heartfelt. Shall I see if I can find something in the diurnal while you speak to the sisters? I can give it to you as you go into chapel.'

'Thank you. That would be such a help.' She took a deep breath and started to move in the direction of the door, but Hugh put his hand out to stop her. 'Will you tell Agnes first? You may have to contain her reaction.'

'And she may pull rank, too,' Lizzie added. 'She is capable of disrupting any service you put together.'

'You're right. I need to see her first, but I don't want her to get to the sisters before I do, as it could all go horribly wrong. Perhaps I can persuade her that it would be good to present a united front to the Community… What time is it?'

'Five o'clock,' he replied. 'You have half an hour to play with.'

'Do you still use the bell for summoning the sisters?' Lizzie asked.

'Yes. The mustering point is just by the front door. It's the same as a fire drill.'

'Well, why don't you gather by the door and then take them into the art room. It's quiet there and you won't be interrupted. After that, you can go straight to the chapel and we'll have the service ready for you.'

'OK, but when shall I speak to Agnes?'

'I think it would be safer to tell her first and then ring the summoning bell. Don't you think?'

'Yes, that makes sense. After I've spoken to them, we'll ring the usual service bell, so you'll know to come. OK?'

'Will you be alright doing that on your own or would you like one of us with you?'

'Thanks for the offer, Lizzie, but it would look odd to have either of you there when I speak to the sisters and I have to learn to face Agnes on my own. If you can work on the service, that will really help.'

'I don't know about the rest of the Community,' Hugh said, when she was gone. 'Does she have any allies?'

'There's Sarah, of course, but I'm not sure about the professed sisters. There used to be twelve of them originally – the number needed to run a small branch house, apparently. Most of the ones I remember have died, but, apart from the Superiors, I think there are six or seven able-bodied sisters – the middle management, as it were. I know there's a Sacristan, a Cook, an Assistant Bursar (taking over from Helena), a Gardener, an Assistant Infirmarian, and there must be others. In fact, I think Thea is their Liturgist – as well as the Sacristan. We should consult her about any new service. Oh God, I don't think I can do this!'

The summoning bell penetrated their reflections with its clamour and Lizzie's voice began to splinter, first with rage and then with pain. Hugh put his arms around her, but she was not to be comforted and pulled away. Instead, she reached for a clipboard and began searching for a form of words that would meet this most terrible need. 'There could be three bodies lined up in that chapel by tomorrow or the next day. Where do we start?' A strange wailing seemed to be coming from somewhere deep inside her and her instinct was to cover her head with her hands as she slumped against the wall. Hugh knew from experience that she needed him to sit close to her, but not try to touch her while the waters went over her head. When she finally put out her arms to him, he was there.

'I think the sisters might need something familiar and

comforting just now, don't you?' he said, after a while, as they sat leaning against the wall, Lizzie enclosed in his arms, her back to his chest. 'If we can put something together from the diurnal, at least we will be in familiar territory. One or two penitential psalms perhaps, but they're going to need something that offers them hope as well. Shall we look together?' He stroked her rich chestnut hair that followed the contour of her head so neatly and persisted in reminding him of the conkers he used to have in his pocket at school.

'Yes,' she said, gratefully, worn out with the tears that had shaken her to the core.

They searched the monastic diurnal together, writing down possible psalms and readings, before Lizzie said, 'I know it should be Vespers, but I think only Compline will do just now. We need something to hold us together.'

'Yes, I think you're right,' he said.

'*Thou shalt not be afraid for any terror by night, nor for the arrow that flieth by day,*' she muttered quietly to herself, the tears pooling in her eyes and overflowing down her cheeks.

They sat together wordlessly until the service bell brought them to their feet. As they made their way towards the nave, Lizzie's hand instinctively sought his and they went in, side by side.

Anastasia was waiting for them in the entrance to the Lady Chapel. As they explained their decision to go for Compline, she nodded her head in assent. 'Good choice. They are all in shock. I don't think they would be able to take in anything else.'

'What did you tell them?'

'The truth. We must learn from this and understand the part we have all played in it. I have asked them all to write down what they think has to change and we will have our own Truth and Reconciliation meetings once the worst is over.'

'How did it go with Agnes?' Hugh asked.

'Strangely unresponsive. It was as if the shutters came down and she was closed for business. Not the least bit interested in the arrangements for the funeral or how the rest of the Community was feeling. She just wanted to know where Magdalen had been shot and if the bullet had touched her face. I asked her if she wanted to take over as Acting Superior and she gave me such an incredulous look that I instinctively stepped back.'

'Shock, I expect,' Hugh said.

'I think it was more than that,' she said firmly. 'It was as if her reason for being here was gone and she was indifferent to everything else.'

'Is she coming to chapel?' Lizzie asked.

'No. She said she would remain in her room till the bodies came back from the post-mortems and would we please have her meals sent up. She implied she had a lot of phoning to do, though she asked me to contact the Bishop Visitor and the various church authorities and register the deaths once we can, so I'm not sure who she was going to contact. Certainly not Anna Sophia's family, as she didn't ask for her mother's care home number.'

'I know you must go in to chapel, but are you OK? It must have taken it out of you to break the news to the sisters.'

'Thanks, Lizzie, but I can't talk now. Shall we meet in the art room after Compline and Supper?'

'Of course. We will be saying Compline with you all – on the other side of the screen.'

Ellen was there, in her usual place when they returned to the nave, looking bloody but unbowed. Presumably, the news had been communicated somehow. They sat down beside her.

CHAPTER TWENTY-FIVE

The wall candles had been lit and there were three flickering tealights lined up on the front of the altar. Otherwise, the chapel was in darkness, as the sisters began the ancient practice of reciting Compline from memory, each in her separate stall. Sarah began with 'Bid sister a blessing' and was answered by Anastasia with 'The Lord Almighty grant us a quiet night and a perfect end.' This was followed by one of the older sisters reciting the familiar short lesson:

'Brethren: be sober, be vigilant, because your adversary the devil, as a roaring lion, walketh about, seeking whom he may devour…'

The Superiors' stalls were all empty.

'What about Sarah?' Hugh whispered to Lizzie. 'Do you think she will stay on and take her final vows, now everything is in such a mess?'

'I think she will,' Lizzie whispered back, making out her familiar figure on the front row of the right-hand stalls, facing Anastasia across the dark expanse of the choir. The atmosphere in the chapel was charged and strangely buoyant, despite the grief and the shock, and for a minute she could see the network of fine connections that held them all up, criss-crossing from side to side like a cat's cradle. The connection between Anastasia and Sarah was particularly strong as they held each other's gaze and answered each other with alternate verses of the psalms.

This is what they do well, Lizzie thought to herself, almost with longing. *This is what makes them strong.* She squeezed Hugh's hand and he gave her a surprised smile, but made no comment.

'I have brought Sarah with me,' Anastasia said, a quarter of an hour later when they gathered in the art room. 'We need to make a plan, I think, and Sarah should be part of it.'

So, this is the new order, Lizzie thought with approval. *No hierarchy. No secrecy. No exclusion of junior sisters and novices...*

'But what about Agnes?' she asked. 'Do you know what line she will take?'

'I have no idea what she is cooking up. She said she had a lot of phoning to do, but she didn't say who.'

'How can she be trusted, after her role in murdering Mother Maria?' Sarah asked.

'Unfortunately, we can't prove that,' Anastasia said, 'and all the witnesses are dead. I suspect the police will just drop the case.'

'But she can't be allowed to carry on, surely?' Sarah said, almost weeping with frustration. 'Don't we have to have an election?'

'Yes, we do. And that is our trump card,' Anastasia said, with a smile.

'But isn't this what Agnes always wanted?' Hugh interrupted. 'I thought her whole plan was centred on being Mother?'

'Yes, it was,' Anastasia replied, 'but that depended on Magdalen being at her side. They were going to run things together and they had such a stranglehold on the Community that they probably would have succeeded, with Maria out of the way.'

'Anna Sophia put a stop to that, though, didn't she?' Lizzie said. 'Her death was not wasted, though it must have felt so at the time. Did you manage to contact her mother?'

'Yes, but I don't know how much she grasped.'

'Did you mention the gun?' Lizzie felt compelled to ask.

'I did, actually, but I just said that she might like to know that her gun had been used in defence of her reputation. She didn't ask for any details and I didn't offer any, but she seemed satisfied.'

'What next then?' Hugh asked, after a pause. 'Can we be of any use? Should we stay on? Should Lizzie stay on?'

'I would be grateful if Lizzie could stay on for a few days until we have the result of the post-mortems and until we know which way Agnes is going to jump,' Anastasia said, turning to Lizzie.

'Of course,' Lizzie said, looking at Hugh to check for his agreement. 'I would like to see it through to the end.'

'I will go then,' Hugh said, enclosing Lizzie in one of his rare bear hugs. 'Look after yourselves – all of you – and remember I am at the end of a phone if you want me.'

Picking up his jacket from the chair, he left quickly and they were on their own.

They all looked to Anastasia, not knowing what to do next. Even the timetable was out of synch, with Compline before Supper and no Vespers. 'I told the sisters we'd have Supper at the usual time,' she said, quickly, 'and I'll tell them to have an early night after that. I think we all need it, don't you?'

It was nearly 7pm, so the three of them joined the queue outside the refectory, grateful for some silence. Anastasia said the opening Latin grace, then explained that Agnes was taking meals in her room for now, so she would lead the Community as the senior sister. She smiled as she added, 'And my first act is to give you all an early night!' There was a ripple of approval from the muted gathering and, for a moment, they all looked a little less lost. Lizzie thought how it would be if they were a family group outside, hit by such a double/triple tragedy, and could see them all gathering in the kitchen over a cup of tea or a glass of wine, having a good rant and a cry, talking it through, making sense of it together. This was not how it worked here. They would take it back to their cells and talk to God about it. Was it better or worse? She didn't know – just that it hadn't worked for her.

As they lined up to process out, Anastasia caught her eye and signed to her to take a detour into the art room. 'Did you notice that Ellen is still here? She must feel like she's trapped in some kind of horror film. Will you come with me to attempt a formal end to the retreat for the two of you? She's in the nave.'

'Certainly.'

Ellen followed Anastasia into the art room with Lizzie at her side, and they both waited for Anastasia to do the impossible and make sense of the recent mayhem.

Anastasia was clearly torn between discretion and openness. In the end, she simply said, 'I'm sorry, Ellen. You should not have been caught up in all this. I hope you will return when we have got things back on an even keel.'

'I have every faith in you, Anastasia,' she replied. 'I have seen the way you have dealt with this horrific situation and I don't think anybody could have done it better. I look forward to seeing the new dispensation next year. I will say goodbye now,' she continued, squeezing Anastasia's arm as she turned to go.

It was a good performance, only slightly marred by her sotto voce comment to Lizzie as she passed, 'I hope you were not mixed up in all this. You were never in your seat when you should have been.' It was said with a smile, but the dagger found its mark.

'Hopefully, she will be discreet when she goes back home,' Anastasia said as the door closed behind her.

'How will it be reported?' Lizzie asked. 'A murder, a suicide and a likely manslaughter. We need to spend some time putting together a coherent narrative – for the Community to make sense of it all and for the Bishop, and the Diocesan Communications Officer when he descends on us, as he certainly will. How are all the deaths connected for a start? Magdalen is the common factor, isn't she?'

'Yes, but there is also Agnes. Things ratcheted up when she arrived. Did she come with a master plan? And what were the dynamics between her and Magdalen? We have assumed that Magdalen was driving things, but maybe it was Agnes. Is that what she wants – to take over the whole thing? She may be setting things up as we speak. We don't know who she's been phoning.'

'Let's talk to her after breakfast tomorrow. It's too late now. And I'm not sure that murder investigations are appropriate for the Greater Silence!'

'No, you're right. I hope you can sleep.'

Lizzie returned to her room in the Sisters' House and tried to put it all together for herself, but the jigsaw wouldn't work without the Agnes-shaped piece.

Instead, she found herself thinking about how they would deal with the bodies once they returned from the hospital or the post-mortems, and what state they would be in. Presumably all three of the bodies would have been kept refrigerated and the main orifices plugged with cotton wool or something, but they would need to be washed and anointed for burial and have the Commendation of a Soul read over them – whatever horrors they had inflicted or endured. She knew she had to be part of it and she owed it to them all for different reasons, but her body and mind recoiled from it, which made her feel ashamed.

She still remembered her reaction to her mother's dead body in the local Chapel of Rest and knew it had to be overcome. She would ask Anastasia. Something told her that she would be at ease with it all.

Meanwhile, the net helpfully revealed that suitable oils for anointing were frankincense and myrrh (no surprise there), spikenard, sandalwood and even cinnamon, with rapeseed oil as a carrier. After that, she felt a bit better prepared and could contemplate sleep. After ringing Hugh to say goodnight, she had a deep bath, infused with her own favourite blend of essential oils – geranium leaf, mandarin and bergamot. And, as ever, she ensured that the depth of the bath was well over the regulation three inches…

CHAPTER TWENTY-SIX

It was departure day under normal circumstances, but, today, breakfast was interrupted by the arrival of Pete Browning and his young assistant, DS Amy Streeter. He was at his officious best and lost no time in informing them that all three bodies would be ready for collection from the hospital morgue by midday the following day, and would require the services of an undertaker.

It was all quite brutal and matter-of-fact and he seemed quite pained to have to tell them that an inquest had been ruled out because the cause of death was undisputed. On the other hand, he was clearly cheered to be able to say that he and DS Streeter would need to interview the other sisters and would require an interview room where they wouldn't be disturbed for the inside of a day. Apparently, they were not pursuing their enquiries concerning Mother Maria's death because the key witnesses and the perpetrators were all dead. Lizzie and Anastasia shared a look at this statement, knowing that Agnes was still at large, but neither of them made any comment and just nodded their assent.

The art room was requisitioned for the day and the tenor of the silence changed tangibly, as the sisters were summoned one by one to give their testimony. The atmosphere felt oppressive, as if all the oxygen had been sucked out of the air, and breathing itself became an effort. The Community did their best to keep their composure but Pete Browning seemed to enjoy breaking up the silence with his loud, impatient voice ricocheting round the hall as he ushered the sisters in and out.

Lizzie found it hard to imagine what questions he was asking them, as he already knew who had done it and why, with three witnesses to prove it. Perhaps he didn't trust the three of them and needed to corroborate their statements, but she doubted that any of the sisters would think it fitting to criticise one of their Superiors or think them capable of blackmail. And it seemed even less likely that they would have an opinion on whether their trusted infirmarian was likely to commit murder or even had a gun in her possession.

They all padded round the same small space in muted fashion – from art room to sacristy to refectory – not meeting each other's eyes and willing the ordeal to be over. Terce was a ragged affair because several sisters were absent, being interviewed or waiting for their turn. Anastasia had little power to stop this intrusion, though she did make it clear to DI Browning that no sisters were to be summoned out of chapel once they were in there.

When coffee time approached, Lizzie and Anastasia took refuge there and began to compare notes. Lizzie's thoughts were already moving to the next day and the laying out that awaited them. She had a vivid memory of the spooky mortuary chapel in the grounds during her time. It was almost an initiation rite for novices to be instructed to keep vigil there in the darkest watches of the night when someone died.

'Do you still use that mortuary chapel?' she asked.

'No, we have a cold room in the infirmary.'

'That's a relief. Who normally does the laying out?'

'It was always Anna Sophia, so I guess it will be me. Will you help me?'

'Of course, though I can't say I relish it! What about Sarah? I think she will want to be a part of it for Maria.'

'Yes, I'm sure you're right.'

'Do you have an undertaker you usually use?'

'Not really, because the sisters normally die in Community. But we do have an Associate who is an undertaker, so we could ask her.'

'Nice that she's a woman.'

'Yes…'

'Let's not lay them out in a row!' Lizzie said, suddenly, teetering on the edge of hysteria. 'It could tip over into farce, couldn't it?!'

'Let's just get started,' Anastasia said, with a reassuring smile. 'It will help to do something practical. I'll ring up Jean, our undertaker friend. She'll know what to do. She's also local, which makes it simpler.'

Jean was surprisingly free and said she would collect the bodies the following morning, before midday office. It was a Sunday, but she seemed unaffected by that. Apparently, they could just use recyclable cardboard coffins, if Anastasia was happy to. All that was needed was measurements. Nothing worse than a body being cramped, apparently.

The bell for Midday Office began to ring just as they were about to bring up the subject of Agnes, so it had to wait. There were only eight sisters in chapel and Lizzie was struck by the decimation of the Community in the last few days. If you counted Helena, it meant there were eight of them left out of the original twelve. A twenty-five per cent death rate! It was beginning to feel like one of those murder mysteries where everybody is incarcerated somewhere for the weekend, then picked off one by one. But what about Agnes? Was she a victim or a perpetrator? They were going to have to beard her in her den – or, at least, Anastasia would have to, if the Community was going to move forward at all.

More of psalm 119 and she was suddenly overwhelmed by the endless stream of words pouring out of the monastic diurnal, trapping them in a status quo that felt feudal. It was all about power and compliance and obedience. Where were the new words? The liberating words that addressed their grief and gave them hope? The new liturgies from Iona, Northumbria, Taizé? Why had the Community not had a liturgical renewal when they changed their habits and opened up their enclosure? Who or what had held them down?

They processed out of chapel soon after and Lizzie waited in the nave for Anastasia. When she arrived, she had Sarah with her, who, as expected, had asked to be part of the preparation of the bodies for burial. She had done it before, apparently, helping Anna Sophia as part of her novitiate training.

Lizzie shook her head at the question in Sarah's eyes and was impressed by the way she held it together and moved straight on to the comment that she would prepare the oils, and have them ready in the cold room on Sunday morning. When Sarah had gone, the two of them shared a rueful look, knowing they could no longer put off the encounter with Agnes.

'Shall we get it over with?' Anastasia asked, leading the way past the Simpering Statue and up the stairs into the Sisters' House. Lizzie followed behind the swish of her habit, noticing how natural it looked on her, whereas she herself had always felt something of an imposter in the habit and veil and was relieved to be back in her customary jeans and jumper.

Agnes' cell was on the same corridor as Maria's and Magdalen's and Anastasia led her straight there. They both paused outside, suddenly apprehensive about what they might find inside. There was no sound coming from the other side and, for a moment, Lizzie had a horrible image of Agnes crouching behind the door with a baseball bat in her hand. 'What are we going to say?' she asked, with barely concealed panic in her voice.

Anastasia's reply was calm: 'The main thing she needs to grasp is that the game is up and she cannot stay on as the Assistant Superior. We will tell her that there will be an election for a new Mother/Leader and she will not be allowed to stand, so any dreams of taking over will have to be abandoned. We can't threaten her with a police investigation, because they have made it clear that the case is closed, but we can let her know that we are aware of her part in the plot and—'

At that moment, the door was wrenched open and a wild-eyed Agnes pulled them both inside. 'I could hear you whispering outside, so come in and tell me to my face!'

There was a case half-open on her bed and she was not wearing her habit, but a strangely old-fashioned tailored suit, which must have been something she arrived in. Her eyes were red-rimmed and her hair was pinned up in a haphazard way. She had obviously been crying.

'I loved her!' she said, half shouting, half crying. 'You never got that, did you? I would have spent the rest of my life with her. I would have done anything, been anyone, to be near her. Do you think I gave a monkey's about being the Mother Superior? This is the last place I want to be without her.'

She was packing frenetically while she was talking, sliding her few personal possessions and toiletries into the case, without taking her eyes off Anastasia and Lizzie.

'Did you never have a vocation for the life? Was it always about Magdalen?' Anastasia asked, at last.

'Of course! She visited the American house when she was young and devastatingly beautiful. I was working there as their accountant and I vowed then that I would find a way to be with her. For a while, I believed I was in love with the life and did my novitiate and took my vows at the American House, but it was always her really. And now she is gone! What have you done with her body? I need to hold her one last time before I go.'

'I'm afraid that won't be possible,' Anastasia said, firmly. 'If you and Magdalen had not plotted to dispose of Maria, none of this terrible chain of events would have been set in motion. We can't prove what you did, but we can at least spare the sisters the torture of your presence at the joint funeral.'

'You are going to give them a joint funeral?' she asked in a horrified tone. 'Those three together, as if they were of equal significance?'

'Yes. Because they are. And the Community needs a dignified space to grieve them all and process the tangled circumstances of their deaths. I'm afraid you will have to do your grieving on your own.'

She moved to go to the door, then turned, with her hand on the handle. 'When are you leaving? Sooner rather than later, I would suggest.'

For once, Agnes was speechless and stood frozen with her hand on the zip of the case, as Lizzie followed Anastasia out. It was a new version of Anastasia emerging, bringing with it a gravitas Lizzie had not seen before. *The grace of office,* she thought to herself, remembering her first encounter with Mother Cicely as a young novice.

Outside in the corridor, Anastasia was quiet, but Lizzie said, 'Do you think it was sexual? And reciprocated?'

'Yes, I do, on both counts. But I don't think it was an equal relationship. I think Magdalen always had the power. You could see it in the way Agnes was always watching her, waiting for her reaction. It wasn't the same the other way round.'

'D'you think she will go today? You don't think we should try and clear up her part in Maria's death?'

'I think that's a hiding to nothing, as my old mother would say. She knows we know she was complicit in the death and she has her punishment, so I think we leave it there. We will be honest with the Bishop when he comes, but we need to put together a press release that will do the least damage to the remaining sisters. The Communications Officer can help us with the appropriate form of words.'

'I doubt if they have a form of words for a double murder and a suicide!' Lizzie smiled, despite herself.

'Good point! Have I got it wrong? D'you think we should hand her over to the police? I just think it would drag things out for the Community, without benefitting anybody. We have no evidence, do we?'

'No, but—'

'The Bishop is coming to see me early this afternoon. I will give him all the facts and ask him what we should do. He will have to do a formal visitation anyway once the funerals are over.'

'OK. See you later.'

Lunch was a buffet again, so there was no queuing and Lizzie was able to make her way to the refectory in her own time, pausing just inside the sacristy to check her phone for any messages. Nothing from Hugh. As she passed through the front hall, the door was half-open and sleet was again falling from a darkening sky. Out of the corner of her eye, she could see a taxi drawing away from the front steps, its occupant sitting very upright and gazing in her direction. Their eyes met and she had a sudden sense of the bleak future awaiting Agnes, but she couldn't bring herself to raise her hand in farewell. Nor could she bring herself to try and stop her. It all seemed irrelevant now. The Community had to find a new way of being and Agnes wasn't part of it.

As she sat in the refectory, relishing her pea and ham soup and fresh bread, she heard the Bishop's voice in the hall and wondered if she ought to inform Anastasia of Agnes' departure, but reminded herself that it was not her business how the diocese presented it all to the world and Anastasia was perfectly capable of handling a Bishop!

She had left a notice on the refectory door, announcing that there would be a Community meeting at 2pm in the art room to discuss the way forward. It was written with her usual warmth and transparency, encouraging the sisters to come and speak openly about their hopes and fears for the future, and Lizzie knew she was witnessing a sea-change in the Community she had once likened to a prison.

DI Browning and DS Streeter seemed to have run out of victims by about 1.45pm and Lizzie enjoyed watching the stand-off between Bishop and Detective Inspector, as they both emerged from their respective rooms at the same time. They were each accompanied by their acolytes, Chaplain and Sergeant respectively, who were immediately faced with a crisis of precedence. Luckily for them, Anastasia joined them in the hall and guided them out together with a sheepdog's unerring instinct. What they said to each other on the other side of the door was anybody's guess, but that was not the Community's problem. They were off the premises and the work of rebuilding could begin.

It was hard to be excluded from such a ground-breaking meeting, but she was invited to tea and cake afterwards in the community room and met a lot of the sisters for the first time. She was immediately drawn to Thea, the Sacristan and Liturgist, who had entered Community late, after a career as a literary agent. She was exciting to talk to, as her love of words was grounded in years of detailed work with her clutch of authors. They talked enthusiastically about a new monastic liturgy for the Community and Lizzie felt sure she would be an ally for Anastasia, as they were also close in age.

The new Infirmarian, Sister Susan Grace, had been a nurse like Anna Sophia, but had none of her exotic background. *Perhaps just as well*, Lizzie thought to herself. She was small and dumpy and obviously felt the cold, as she was encased in several layers of teal-coloured waistcoats and cardigans, and even a woolly scarf round her neck instead of the collar. She looked about seventy-five, but could have been younger.

Anastasia introduced her to Sister Edith, the new Bursar, over some homemade carrot cake, and Lizzie listened attentively as she expressed her concerns for the correct governance of the Community. She was forcibly reminded of the Belbin test they had been subjected to in her counselling training and the importance of a 'Completer-Finisher' in every team. Edith would keep them straight, she knew, but she didn't have Helena's sardonic humour, so Lizzie was not inclined to linger.

The cake was clearly a great hit with all the sisters and it seemed clear that the Community meeting had been a success because their heads were up and they were making eye contact with each other at last. Lizzie glanced in Sarah's direction to check that she was alright, but she seemed so much in her element, handing the cake round and replenishing the tea, that she felt able to leave them to it and slip away. Picking up her coat from her room across the corridor, she escaped down the garden stair for one last time. The urge to go outside, even if it was still sleeting, was too strong to resist. The need to say her farewells to the hermitage, the garden, even the high wall that wrapped around the building and enclosed the Community, took her outside and marked her steps.

Her feet took her unerringly to the hermitage, where she lit a candle and sat on the stone bench, listening to the silence. There was little or no wind and just a fine sleety snow falling.

It had been a very odd route to inner peace, but something had definitely shifted inside her. She felt as if it might take days or even months to process it all, and remembered almost nostalgically the seven-day silent retreat she had been required to do before her first profession. It had felt then as if she had sunk to a level of consciousness deeper than words and even physical sensation, which was like a rich, fecund soil – healing and restorative. She needed that now and sat there without moving until she heard the bell for Vespers.

CHAPTER TWENTY-SEVEN

After breakfast the next morning, she went back to her room and began to put things in her case. They were having a Eucharist at 10.30am as it was Sunday, so she had missed Lauds and had a late morning. It still felt quite wicked, but she was working on it. Anastasia greeted her with a smile when she came down into the hall from the Sisters' House and was just about to ask her something when there was a commotion at the front door. They both turned to see Jean at the top of the steps, asking where they would like the coffins delivered. She was early, but Anastasia was immediately in practical mode. 'Could you drive round to the infirmary, please, Jean? We have a cold room there, ready to receive them.'

As Jean drove off, Lizzie said, 'Shall I alert Sarah? She will be in the sacristy, won't she?'

'Yes. Tell her the coffins have arrived and we will meet to do the laying out after lunch. I will go and receive the bodies at the infirmary.'

'OK.'

Sarah was indeed in the sacristy, cleaning out the candlesticks like a normal day. They had a brief conversation about the arrangements before Lizzie returned to the front hall, thinking she could squeeze in a quick coffee before the service. It was 10.10am.

Someone – probably Sarah – had kindly put the coffee urn on early and she sat with her steaming mug in a corner of the deserted refectory, trying to piece together the order of events since her arrival on Tuesday. It felt like a very long journey, as if she had been there for centuries rather than the inside of a week. Outside, she could hear the sound of traffic and voices raised in conversation and greeting. A normal day. She was aware of the anxiety building inside her at the thought of what was to come after lunch, but knew there was no avoiding it, though she recoiled from the thought of seeing the untenanted bodies of two people she had loved so much.

All the same, it seemed fitting that the last lesson she needed to learn should come through the body. She thought back to the first weeks of her novitiate and how hard her Protestant soul (neck, even) had found it to do the deep bow to the reserved sacrament on entering chapel, but how it had gradually taught her reverence. And the same for humility, with the knocking on doors, however perverse that felt. Even the absence of coffee except on feast days had taught her a sober lesson. The current sisters didn't know they were born, having good coffee on tap at all times!

As she washed up her mug, she knew that the cycle was almost complete and she would be able to leave this time without looking back, maybe even visit in the future and be a witness to the Community's new life.

The bell for the Eucharist was sounding, which brought Sarah to mind as she would be on the end of the bell rope, and she looked once more at her phone, hoping to see in her inbox the news she knew Sarah craved. Nothing there.

Anastasia was celebrating at the altar, resplendent in her embroidered purple vestments, and Sarah was her thurifer, making a great job of filling the chapel with incense. The smoky atmosphere and the very particular smell took Lizzie straight back to her own time as chapel novice and that sense of charged anticipation that Advent always brought. Much better than the increasingly commercial run-up to Christmas 'outside', but then Christmas Day in the Community had always felt so lonely without her family around. She hugged the thought of Hugh to herself and realised again how close she had been to desolation and despair before they had found each other.

The sisters looked as if they were able to relax at last, as if they had found their place again and it was a happy sight.

Midday office and lunch followed quite quickly and soon the last office was over and the last meal finished, and it was time to go over to the infirmary. The first thing Lizzie noticed when she opened the door from the covered way was the incense and how much its rich, spicy smell permeated the building. Anastasia had been busy. There were also candles on every windowsill – in the lobby and the corridor, as well as the cold room, which had its door partly open at the end of the corridor, beyond the pharmacy and Maria's room.

Anastasia and Sarah were already there, kitted out in plastic aprons and latex gloves. The coffins were still closed. As Lizzie put on her own apron and gloves, Sarah explained, in her most professional voice, what would happen next. 'We will use this bed here. The mattress has a wipe-down surface and it will be covered each time with a clean linen sheet before we lift the body onto it. Maria died in the hospital, so her body will have been washed and the orifices plugged to prevent leakage of bodily fluids. It is likely to be a different story with Magdalen and Anna Sophia…'

Sarah paused for a second and Anastasia gently interrupted: 'I think we are agreed that our main focus is to anoint their bodies for burial, with the same respect and tenderness that the two Marys accorded Jesus in the Gospels. The oils and spices we have made up are as close to the biblical ones as we could find – frankincense and myrrh, spikenard, a little cedarwood, all mixed with a carrier oil. We can use a linen shroud and infuse that with the oils, too, if you think that would be the right course, but my feeling is that we just dress them in the habit and let them be…'

They both nodded their assent and she continued, 'Shall we start with Anna Sophia? I think we might find her the most challenging.'

The coffins bore their names and they lifted her carefully onto the bed, as they all braced themselves for how she might look. Her eyes were closed, which spared them the sight of one eyeball hanging out, and the pathology technician had clearly worked hard to suture the wound in her cheekbone and patch up the shards of bone, so that she was still recognisably Anna Sophia.

They all looked at her bruised and battered face and Sarah's first instinct was to wash it with the rose water that lay to hand and dry it with a clean white towel, then Anastasia put her thumb deep into the pot of oils and spices and made the sign of the cross on her forehead. She followed this up by anointing the palms of her hands and the soles of her feet in the same way.

The aromatic spices lingered around her body like a blessing, as the three of them worked together, dressing her in a clean habit, with the pectoral cross placed in her hands at the centre of her chest.

Once she had been lowered gently into her coffin, it was time to decide who was next. 'D'you think Maria now?' Anastasia said, carefully, looking at Sarah. 'Are you ready?'

'Yes. Let's do it.'

Together, they lifted their old friend and laid her on the clean linen sheet, Sarah at her head and Anastasia and Lizzie at her feet. Her body was grey, and cold and clammy to the touch, as Jean had warned them it would be, but there was no longer any rigor mortis, so her limbs were soft and easy to manipulate, almost floppy. Her face still retained traces of the 'beatific smile' Anna Sophia had reported seeing at her death, which clearly made Sarah very happy, and she kissed her cold forehead before asking Anastasia if she could be the one to anoint her head.

Permission granted, she made the sign of the cross in the middle of Maria's forehead as she whispered goodbye and Godspeed, tenderly infusing her flesh with the rich, spicy oils. Anastasia then anointed the palms of her hands and the soles of her feet and Lizzie said her own farewells by making the sign of the cross on her friend's breastbone, close to her heart, sad in the knowledge that she could not have put her own lips to the cold flesh.

They dressed her in her old-style habit and veil, as they knew she had requested, and, against all tradition, put the Reverend Mother's antique gold ring on the fourth finger of her right hand.

'We don't usually bury the sisters with any jewellery,' Anastasia said, quietly, 'but it seems the right way to honour her. Don't you think?'

They both nodded in agreement as they lifted Maria's body into her coffin.

Now comes the worst part, Lizzie thought, as her heart started to race. *Just don't faint*, she said to herself, as they took the lid off Magdalen's coffin and lifted her onto the bed.

The first thing she noticed was that her hair was wet and dishevelled. Lizzie knew she wouldn't have liked to be seen with her hair out of place and instinctively began to comb it. 'They sometimes hose down the bodies after a post-mortem,' Sarah said. 'It's not pretty, is it?'

There were large stitches in a great arc across her chest, but she was otherwise untouched and the perfection of her face and body was there to see, except it was like looking at a statue carved in alabaster. *Ichabod,* Lizzie whispered to herself, *the glory has departed.*

Her heart rate had slowed down and she felt completely calm. Anastasia and Sarah were both clearly struggling to come to terms with what Magdalen had done. 'She looks so unruffled,' Sarah said, 'as if nothing has touched her, when she caused such mayhem!'

'I know,' Anastasia said. 'I don't understand how she could live with her conscience.'

'I think she was a very damaged person,' Lizzie responded. 'Anna Sophia told me that it was her father's love she wanted and never got, because he couldn't forgive her for killing her mother.'

'Killing her mother?' Anastasia said in disbelief, as she prepared to administer the oils.

'Yes, in childbirth. She was an artist apparently and very beautiful. Magdalen grew to be like her but not till she was much older. He sent her away and never looked at her again until she began to be feted for her beauty and accomplishments.'

'So, getting the top job would make him notice? And perhaps love her?'

'Anna Sophia said so. Yes.'

'Well, I hope they meet in heaven and they are both forgiven.'

Their eyes met over Magdalen's body and silence fell, as each in her own way contemplated the complexity of forgiveness. The silence was broken by Lizzie asking, 'May I?' At a nod from Anastasia, she made the sign of the cross on Magdalen's forehead and whispered a phrase that Magdalen had always used to her when they parted in the early days: *Go Under the*

Mercy. Something in that phrase opened the floodgates and she found herself weeping silently as Anastasia gravely completed the anointing, and the three of them dressed her in all her finery and placed the pectoral cross in her hands over her heart.

'You loved her, despite all, didn't you?' Anastasia said, as they braced themselves to lift the dead weight. *Our strength is all gone into heaviness,* she thought, remembering Cleopatra and her maidservants trying to lift the dying Anthony up onto her monument. 'Yes,' she said.

'This is where we read the Commendation over them all,' Anastasia said as they fixed the coffin lids. 'I will just do the short form.' They all opened their monastic diurnals and followed as she read:

'I commend thee to Almighty God, dearest sisters, and commit thee to him whose creatures thou art; that when thou hast paid the debt of all mankind by dying, thou mayest return to thy Maker, who formed thee from the dust of the earth. When therefore thy soul goeth forth from the body, may the shining company of Angels await thee; may the adjudging council of Apostles meet thee; may the triumphant army of white-robed martyrs come forth to welcome thee…'

At this point, Lizzie tuned out and let the words wash over her, wilfully ignoring the lily-crowned confessors and the choir of exulting virgins, as she always had. *This is where I came in,* she thought, with a smile, *and it's time to go.*

Anastasia was coming to an end as she refocused on the reading. 'The coffins will remain here until the funeral tomorrow. And when that is done, we can perhaps get on with the business of rebuilding!' she said, with a return of her old, brisk pragmatism, closing and locking the door behind her as she spoke.

'I suppose the election will have to be next?' Sarah asked, as they walked back along the covered way.

'Yes and your life profession. I think we can waive the usual three-years' wait, if you are sure.'

'I am sure. And I would like to add the name *Maria* and call myself "Sarah Maria" from then on.'

'Perfect!' Anastasia said, turning to her with a big grin on her face. 'Yes! Mother Maria lives on!' Lizzie said, pumping the air in triumph.

She decided not to stay for the funeral, though she heard it was rather grand and rather extraordinary to have three bodies all 'done' at once. She had no doubt that if Anastasia was in charge, they would all have been dispatched with a certain panache. There were not exactly balloons apparently, but she had constructed banners to fly over each of the coffins – illustrated with individual heraldic animals, and each bearing the line from the Song of Songs, in her elegant calligraphy: *And his banner over me was love.* Sarah played *The Sky Boat Song* on her clarinet, to speed them on their way.

CHAPTER TWENTY-EIGHT

She had been home a week when the email and letter arrived, confirming that Sarah was Maria's daughter. She immediately drove back to the convent and asked to see Sarah personally, but she was in chapel where her profession ceremony was taking place, so she simply readdressed the envelope with the name Sister Sarah Maria and left it with the portress, closing the door quietly behind her.

Pausing by the gate, she looked back at the high sandstone buildings, in all their forbidding grandeur, and thought to herself, *The spell is broken.*

Before getting in her car, she had one last look down at the river and up at the mountains beyond, remembering how as a novice she used to hide out in the attic bathroom to catch a glimpse of the mountains. *Don't fence me in* would be forever associated with that cold attic bathroom. Later, it was the loss of the songs and the draining away of her identity that drove her to sing Bob Dylan and Leonard Cohen to herself as she swept the sanctuary carpet. *Knockin' on Heaven's Door* and *So Long, Marianne* and all the other songs kept her sane, as they still did.

The sun was glinting on the wide river below as it wound its way through the meadows on the outskirts of the old border city, but her heart was driving her back to the mountains and home. She went the back way, avoiding the motorway, so that she could hug the side of Blencathra for as long as possible as she drove through Caldbeck and Mosedale and along the valley bottom until she reached Mungrisdale, the open moorland, and home. *The mountain sat upon the plain/In his tremendous chair,* she chanted gleefully to herself as she put the key in the door and headed for the kitchen and a long overdue coffee.

That evening, over a celebratory meal of chicken cooked in white wine, cream and tarragon, and a bottle of the finest Chablis, Hugh said, 'Is it over? Are you free?'

'Yes, I actually think I am. When we finished anointing them, I felt something lift in me, so even if we get another lockdown, as seems likely, I think I'll be OK.'

'Thank God for that!' he said, squeezing her hand across the table. 'Christmas is on then?'

Later, as they watched one of their favourite Nordic noirs on the TV, Hugh said, looking straight ahead, 'Would you have been able to forgive her if she hadn't been shot?'

'I don't know. I've been thinking about it a lot. Her death was shocking, but there was something disturbingly clean about it. Almost as if the account had been settled and we could all move on.'

'Why "disturbing"?'

'Because it feels primitive. Old Testament stuff.'

'More like Greek tragedy to me. *Hubris* and *nemesis*.'

'But what about forgiveness? We should be able to do forgiveness without retribution,' she said in a bleak voice.

'I think Anastasia and the Community would have managed it, don't you?' he said, raising his eyes to hers.

'But what if she hadn't really been repentant, or not even

grasped that she needed to be repentant – there would always have been a festering wound. How could they live with that?'

'I think your old friend Leonard would have something to say about that, don't you? Wasn't there something about cracks letting the light in?' he said, with a sneaky smile, as he headed for the fridge and another bottle of wine.

'You can't get out of it that easily,' she said, following him and pushing him up against the kitchen cupboard, then wrapping her arms tightly around him…

AUTHOR'S NOTE

Although as a young woman I spent five years in a religious community, the novel that follows is not autobiographical and the characters are entirely fictitious. I did not witness a murder and only heard about the tragic suicide of a novice at third hand.

I am, however, very aware that the story emerged out of my unconscious after many years of grappling with the disturbing themes that were around at that time and seem to recur wherever there is an imbalance of power in a religious context.

All liturgical quotations are taken from *The Monastic Diurnal,* OUP, London & New York, 1956 edition